"Fake Geek Girl" originally published in Review of Australian Fiction ©2015.

"Unmagical Boy Story" originally published on the Sheep Might Fly podcast ©2016

"The Bromancers" originally published on the Sheep Might Fly podcast ©2017

"The Alchemy of Fine" originally published as a Patreon exclusive ebook ©2017

ISBN: 978-0-6484370-7-9 ebook

ISBN: 978-0-6484370-8-6 print

❀ Created with Vellum

UNREAL ALCHEMY

TANSY RAYNER ROBERTS

CONTENTS

FAKE GEEK GIRL

UNMAGICAL BOY STORY

THE BROMANCERS

THE ALCHEMY OF FINE

HOLIDAY BREW (BELLADONNA U #2)

FAKE GEEK GIRL

CHAPTER 1
HEBE + PHOENIX BOY = OTP

MY SISTER HOLLY is a fake geek girl. A card-carrying, blatant, "I pretend to care about superheroes to get attention in public" fake geek girl.

It's not like the world doesn't know this. Her friends know. My friends know. The fans of her band know, though I suspect a lot of them assume that the name of the band is ironic.

Maybe I should start again.

Holly Hallow is the lead singer of a band called Fake Geek Girl. You might have heard of them - at the very least, you've probably seen the vid of "Witches Roll Dice, Bitches," which went viral last summer, and there are quotes from their classic song "Someone Is Wrong On the Internet" all over Tumblr and Mirrorweb.

If you go to Belladonna University, there's no question that you've heard of the band. They play every Friday night down at Medea's Cauldron, and whether you're in the College of the Real or the College of the Unreal, you've seen my sister screaming out at you from one of the flyers posted around campus.

I couldn't do that. Holly's been singing in public since we turned four, when no one got to the 'Happy Birthday' song early enough in the party for her liking and she turned it into a 30 minute solo. I hate attention. I hate people looking at me. If I had my own way I would slide through life, three steps behind Holly, deep and safe in her shadow. It's comfortable there. I have snacks, and a reading list.

Before you ask (and everyone always asks, once they figure it out), I really don't mind that everything important in my life has been turned into one of Holly's geektastic songs. I don't mind that whenever she hangs out with me and my friends, it's to catch up on the memes and games and trending topics and everything we care about, so she can pour it into lyrics.

Her drummer is one of my best friends in the world. Sage was my first boyfriend, and the reason we broke up is Fake Geek Girl's third most popular song of all time. If I wasn't okay with all this, I would have moved to Bolivia by now. Or Mars.

No, the part that bothers me is that it's really hard to be a dedicated wallflower when your IDENTICAL TWIN SISTER is a campus celebrity. An openly bisexual, super confident campus celebrity, whose public persona screams 'approach me, buy me drinks, hey let's flirt a little.'

Conversations like the one that happened today in the Desiree O'Dowd Unreal Library are pretty much a daily occurrence for me.

PRETTY BOY WITH PHOENIX TATTOO: Hey, Last Straight Girl in the City.

HEBE (sighing loudly): I'm not her.

PHOENIX BOY: Okay...

HEBE: You saw the band, right?

PHOENIX BOY: Yeah, last Friday night at the Cauldron. You were brilliant, I really liked...

HEBE: Still not her. Holly Hallow is my twin sister. I'm Hebe.

PHOENIX BOY: You're not the Fake Geek Girl singer.

HEBE: No, I just look like her.

PHOENIX BOY: Is this a thing you say to avoid groupies?

HEBE (cracks up laughing because I do still have a sense of humour about this): Bonus points for use of the word 'groupies' to describe yourself.

PHOENIX BOY: Hey, I call it like I see it.

HEBE (shows him wallpaper of my phone, which is a pic of me and Holly together, for the specific purpose of proving to people I am not lying about having an identical twin sister): There we go.

PHOENIX BOY: Whoa. Twins. Can you sing too?

HEBE: Nope.

PHOENIX BOY (truth dawning on him): You're the sister. Like, the sister from Time Agents Stole My Sister and Big Gay Break Up Song?

HEBE: Wow, you really stayed for the whole set list.

PHOENIX BOY: It's a great band.

HEBE: Yes, it is. I'm very proud of her. You can go now.

PHOENIX BOY: You're like her muse. You're the first muse I've ever met.

HEBE: Literally no one has ever said that to me ever.

PHOENIX BOY: Is that a lie?

HEBE: No, it's sarcasm. Please stop now.

I related this conversation word for word to Sage and Mei over takeaway noodles in Sage's kitchen that night. I wasn't entirely sure they were listening. Mei always has at least one laptop and two mirrors open, and Sage had three Theoretical Sorcery textbooks spread across the kitchen counter, trying to make sticky notes attach to the pages.

Real books hate contact with the Unreal, so he was on to a losing streak with the sticky notes, but Sage isn't brilliant at listening to advice until he's tried and failed every single option for himself. Which actually explains our entire high school relationship, but there you go.

The point is, neither of them were properly listening, which was good because it allowed me to rant without consequence. Or so I thought.

"I think you should have given him a break," said Mei, still typing as she talked.

"You're not mirroring this conversation, are you?" I asked suspiciously. Never trust a woman who is an expert in both Real and Unreal social media — and believes that privacy is an outdated concept.

"Of course not." She looked up at me, and I saw dialogue reflected in her glasses. Mei is a Big Name Fan in about three different media fandoms, and has several major fic deadlines going at any one time. When she stops multitasking, that's when you've got to worry. "Sounds like he was flirting with you."

"No," I said patiently. "He was flirting with Holly. Everyone flirts with Holly. Holly is so amazing at being flirted with, she doesn't even have to be in the same room at the time."

I felt the soft buzz of magic from the other side of the room as Sage coated the sticky notes in a Real aura. It flicked off, plastering itself to his shirt. Magical clothes developing independent personalities, that was totally what they needed in this flat.

"Mei's right," said Sage. "He stayed to talk after he found out who you are. The trouble with you, Hebes, is you're so used to thinking of Holly as the cool one, you don't even notice when people are into you."

"I had to sneak up on you to become your friend," Mei said with a solemn nod. "I stalked you online for a year before you accepted that we were always going to eat lunch together until time stops and the world ends."

I nudged her with my foot. "You're adorable."

"See what you nearly missed out on?" She indicated her Athena Owl t-shirt and sparkly purple sneakers. "By a narrow margin."

They both had a point, but that didn't mean they were right

in this specific instance. "I think perhaps I failed to describe quite how outrageously attractive this boy was."

"No, that came across," said Mei with an impish smile.

"He was like — magical royalty. Posh foreign accent. There may have been a silk shirt and a phoenix tattoo. Antique sigils on a pendant. And — you know." I shifted uncomfortably. "Muscles."

The boys who are interested in me once they get to know me are not boys who look like that.

Sage rolled his eyes at me. "He's a fan of the band, Hebes. That means he's into your brain."

"I'm not in the band," I said sulkily.

"Half our songs are about you, dimwit. You basically ARE the band."

It was an odd thought, and one I hadn't entertained before. But before I could question him further, he added one spell too many to the precarious sticky notes disaster, and they exploded in his hands.

Magical confetti rained down on us from above, and in our attempts to protect all of the electronic devices in the flat, the conversation was forgotten.

————

WEDNESDAY

"So *you* must be Holly."

I can see how he made that leap. When I work in the Desiree O'Dowd I dress in full librarian chic — all cardigans and retro A-line skirts. I even put my hair up in a bun because come on, how could I not? Working in a library. Living the dream.

On the other hand, when I work at the student advice centre, I dress in whatever I've picked off my floor that morning, and they're lucky if I remember to turn the t-shirt the right way out. Add to this I had a pink wash in my light-brown hair (I lost a bet with my sister, who wanted me to try it out to see if she could risk the look for Friday night) and sure, I can buy that he thought I was the other twin this time around.

But that didn't stop me saying "Still Hebe," in a put-upon sigh, because the only fun thing about being a twin is making people feel guilty about getting it wrong.

It was him again. The pretty boy with the phoenix tattoo that wrapped around the side of his neck and occasionally blew real-istic-looking flames across his medium-brown skin. To his credit, he looked crestfallen at his mistake. I'm guessing he wasn't used to anyone telling him he was wrong.

"Shit. I'm sorry I — really? You work here too?"

"Part-time jobs are precarious things," I told him gravely. "So many students fighting over minimum wage shifts — it's a jungle out there. I juggle multiple jobs to cover rent and food and books."

I had been right about him being Real Royalty — instead of the 'I know your pain' grimace of a fellow working student, he had a baffled 'wait there are students whose parents don't cover all their living costs?' twitch across three quarters of his beau-tiful face.

I was pretty sure his jacket cost more than my monthly rent.

"Right," he said, taking a deep breath. "Can we start again?"

"Any time you're ready," I said sweetly.

Okay, I'll admit that I sometimes enjoy the phenomenon that I refer to as the Hollyfluster. Yes, it's annoying to be constantly hit on by people who think my sister is super cool. But once they have opened a conversation with that, I feel no remorse at all about being sarcastic at them.

Normally I'd be nervous and fumbling around a pretty, privi-leged Real boy (not that one would bother to talk to me without the Holly factor) but right now I was having fun.

Then I felt bad almost straight away, because Phoenix Boy was looking shifty and uncomfortable, and oh crap, he had a genuine problem he had come here to fix, and here was me teasing him because he couldn't tell the difference between twin sisters.

"Starting again," I said, more gently than before. "What do you need?"

"I need to know the process for switching my degree from Real to Unreal," he blurted out.

I lost all ability to be neutrally helpful, and just stared at him. "Seriously?"

"Do I not look serious? I'm uh, asking for a friend," he added, with a practiced tilt of his head that didn't fool me at all.

"Okay," I said slowly. "Well, the process is pretty simple. I can print you out the form here, or you can download it off the website. You need to see a course advisor and get signatures of the Dean from each college. I mean, your friend — I can make an appointment for them with Sarah, she's the course advisor on duty over the summer. Or they can email her directly." I handed him Sarah's business card, because I wasn't sure he was going to give up the 'it's for a friend' story any time soon."

Phoenix Boy looked at the card, and not at me. When he finally turned his dark brown eyes up to fix on my face, my stomach almost entirely melted out of my body. Yes, he was that pretty, shut up.

"But?" he invited.

"But nothing. Straightforward. Forms. Appointments. Signatures."

"But," he said, more forcefully than before.

"It's not common, that's all. But I've only been working here a year…"

I'd never heard of a single transfer between Real and Unreal. A couple, yes, going the other way — because studying magic and its related disciplines was always a safe job-friendly choice and the romance of specialising in magic-free arts or politics or literature often wore off once the careers fair destroyed everyone's hopes and dreams.

But who would give up studying magic once it had its hooks into you? And why would a boy who looked like an illustrated chapter in the history of pampered legacy kids make that choice?

Maybe it really was advice for a friend.

"We also have counsellors," I found myself blurting out.

"General feelings counsellors. If that's something you think would be useful."

Phoenix Boy smiled at that point, though it wasn't a happy or relieved smile. It was a 'you can't make my day worse than it was before I saw you' kind of smile.' "I'm good. I'll take a printed copy of that transfer form. And do you know where I can go to look for accommodation options?"

I waved at the general direction of the bulletin board. "It's probably too late to register for a room in one of the residential halls, but there's a bunch of flatmate and share-house requests over there."

I was going to make up for my previous utter lack of professionalism by leaving it at that, and I totally wasn't going to draw attention to one flatshare flyer in particular, but Phoenix Boy found it anyway. Unsurprising, since Sage and Dec had been up half the night decorating the flyers with fierce fluoro pens, and had insisted I use pins shaped like tiny battle-axes to attach it to the board.

"Join the Manic Pixie Dream House," Phoenix Boy read aloud with a bemused tone in his voice. "Must be able to endure one flatmate's long drumming sessions, and the other flatmate's constant smell of wet art materials (mostly clay). Brace yourself for meals made mostly of dead animal, and weekend gaming marathons in which the flat fills up with angry nerdboys and rattling dice."

"They're friends of mine," I admitted.

"Do they have mixed feelings about letting someone else share the flat with them?"

I laughed, the weird tension of the help desk finally leaving the conversation. "They're not quite hauling up a drawbridge, but they don't want another disaster — that's pretty much a list of reasons why their last flatmate flipped out and stuck them with his share of the rent with no notice."

"Ouch," said Phoenix boy, still staring at the flyer. "Are they — students of the Real or the Unreal?"

"One of each."

That surprised him. He spun around and stared at me, as if

the idea of a mixed household was completely off the chart crazy. "Seriously?"

"It's not that unusual," I said, blinking. Just how sheltered was this boy? Had he never had a friend from the College of the Unreal before? I wasn't sure whether to throw him at Sage and Dec for his own sake, or warn him off their chaos.

"Huh," was all he said, and when he walked away with the transfer forms, he took a tab from the Manic Pixie Dream House with him.

CHAPTER 2

SAGE DOESN'T HATE KARAOKE NIGHT (BUT HE'S NOT GONNA SING)

THURSDAY

So I HEARD this rumour that most universities don't have an all night coffee house like Cirque De Cacao to rely on for their karaoke needs?

Man, most universities must suck.

Cirque De Cacao is smack dab between the Real and Unreal campuses. You'd think it'd mostly be Unreal students cos of the screwy effects that coffee has on magic, but the manager was sensible enough to set up a serious hot chocolate menu to lure in the witches who don't want to face down their senior tutors next morning with a caffeine hangover sucking all the Real from their veins.

Assuming that magic is stored in our veins. I never really thought about that. Maybe it's in the pores.

Me, I was raised in an anti-magic household, and I'd been drinking hardcore espressos since I was eleven, so maybe it's not a surprise that I didn't know about my affinity for Advanced Real Engineering until I tested off the charts at the end of high school.

These days, I limit coffee drinking to uni holidays, and when I'm sick of making the TV go fzzzt-bang just by being in the same room as me. But it was still weeks before the new semester started, and that meant I could drink a cappuccino without fucking up my grades.

Unfortunately, it also made me a Holly magnet.

"Sage Sage Sage Sage!" Three seconds after Skinny Goth Waiter served my drink, Holly whipped into the booth opposite me and leaned over so far that her nose nearly dabbed into the chocolate-dusted froth in my cup. "Omigod that smells amazing."

"Get your own," I said, batting at her with a napkin.

"Can't, I have to visit the Mums tonight so they don't fuss about me and Hebes staying in town again this weekend, and train tickets are wicked expensive. Gonna have to be the broom."

I gave her a flat look. "Hol, you can't fly straight at the best of times. That sound like a dumbarse idea."

"Yeah," she admitted, chewing on a fingernail. "If I hitch-hike instead of broomstick, I can have a coffee now. I really want a caramel macchiato."

"You're not hitch — huh." I glared at her. "Yeah, you can borrow my car."

Holly gave me her rock star smile, the one that makes her glow like she's singing this song for You And No One Else. A lot of blokes and even more girls have done stupid things because of that smile, and I wish I could say I wasn't one of them.

Seriously, I'm not even attracted to girls, and she is my least favourite girl who looks exactly like she does, so how does she get away with this every frigging time?

"Thank you, Sage," she crooned, picking up a coffee stirrer from the end of the table, and drawing a heart in my foam.

"Next time just fucken ask."

"So," Holly said, moving on to the next topic with a gleam in her eye. "I hear you have a hot new flatmate, which means *we* have a hot new housemate."

"How did you know about that? It happened an hour ago." She claims getting the gossip is not her magic power, but all of our mates know better than to try and keep a secret from Holly.

That one time we set up a surprise party for her, she got to the place an hour before we did and scared the hell out of Hebe when she arrived with the cake.

That went down in history as the 'Five Second Rule is extended to Ten Seconds When Cake Is Involved' Party. We all swore we'd never do it again.

"It's true, then?" she said eagerly. "You *do* know who he is?"

"Of course I know who he is, I just met him and agreed he could have Matteus's old room for the semester. I wanna know how you know who he is."

"Ferdinand Chauvelin," she said with relish. "He's one of the Basilisk Kings."

I winced. "Shit, Holly. Why'd you have to tell me that?"

The Basilisks were the founders of the College of the Real — some of the most powerful warlocks in Aussie history. Their kids (grandkids now, as the new generation takes hold) get automatic entry to the hallowed halls. So of course, they swan around acting like they own the place.

After spending the last two years keeping my head down and avoiding all that legacy politics bullshit, I'd gone and let it into my flat. Sure, I'd figured that Ferd had a 'born with a silver dragon in his mouth' kinda vibe, but Basilisk King was a whole different bag of dice.

"I'm not holding that against him," I went on, refusing to let Holly get to me. "Bloke's all right, a bit jumpy, that's all. He's got a crush on Hebes."

That had been the best part of the roommate interview, when Dec managed to get the new bloke to admit he had heard about our place because of the pretty girl at Student Services. The revelation that she was my ex girlfriend and yes hey, I was the drummer in that band, and yes that song is about me and Hebe, and… let's just say that Dec was cackling like a mad goblin by the end of it, and I'd given up on awkward explanations and had gone all the way to laughing like a drain.

Better Ferd knew what he was getting into now, with our crazy incestuous little group.

"On Hebe?" Holly's face lit up like an enchanted toadstool

on the really good drugs. The matchmaking force is strong with this one.

"Full on crush. Hearts in his eyes." I was throwing Hebe under the bus here, but if Holly was concentrating on fixing her sister up with the new bloke, she might lay off spreading all his dirty laundry around campus.

I had underestimated her. She shrugged off my distraction technique and doubled down on gossip. "Remember last year when there was some kind of explosion in the Thaumaturgery and a student ended up in hospital? I think it was him. Ferdinand Chauvelin."

That was worthy of a blank stare. I call it my drummer wall because it's (apparently) the expression I get some time into the second set when I can't think of anything but the beat. It's great for being vaguely intimidating to anyone who isn't Holly. "Do I even want to know why that's your working theory?"

"Well, I know he's friends with that bitch Viola Vale – you know the one, she's like the Basilisk High Galactic Empress — and Jules Nightshade, too. Both of them went really quiet on social media after it happened, and Juniper heard that Omar said…"

"Wow," I said and drank some coffee. My Real senses unwound and faded to black as my body took in the hot milk and the caffeine. "Your brain, Holly."

"It's mostly Facebook," she said modestly. "The new app on Mirrorweb is amazing."

I shook my head at her. "You have time to stalk a complete stranger across computers and mirrors but you don't have time to watch that box set of *The Bromancers* I lent you?"

She rolled her eyes at me. "Sage, no one who has a life has time to watch a box set of anything."

"You are the worst person I have ever met."

"I know," she smiled happily. "So, what can you tell me about this Ferdinand who apparently is going to marry my sister and make beautiful magical nerd babies with her?"

I gulped more of my coffee down, because Holly was still

looking like she might stick her face entirely into the cup. "He just walked in the door. Ask him yourself."

———

FERD CHAUVELIN NEEDED HELP. That much was obvious. Holly and our bandmate Juniper had dragged the poor bastard to the comfy velvet couches in the corner of Cirque de Cacao and were practically in his lap. He looked completely bemused as two thirds of Fake Geek Girl grilled him about his life, his past, his future, and all kinds of things he obviously didn't want to talk about.

I could have rescued him, but I wasn't gonna, because Holly had left her phone on the table and...

Okay, I'm not proud of this.

I was reading her messages.

Ferd was a hell of a distraction, but he was by no means the most important thing happening to us this week — and by us I mean the band. And me. And Holly. And...

It's complicated, okay? But I had to know what the hell was going on, and short of actually having a shouting match with her (it might start out as a conversation but it was going to end up with us screaming at each other if my suspicion was right) this was the best way.

Good thing I drank the coffee earlier. Without it suppressing my abilities, I wouldn't just have exploded the phone, I probably would have brought the whole cafe down around our ears.

Because, yeah. Suspicion confirmed. Shit.

Holly came back to the table, breathless and beaming. I slipped her phone under a napkin so she wouldn't see what I was up to. "It's all fixed," she announced. "Ferd's going to sing in the second set, so you have to as well, I know you hate karaoke night..."

"I don't hate karaoke night, I just hate how many people sing our songs to attempt some kind of stealth audition because they know we're gonna be here. And I'm not singing. No way."

Holly's phone went off. My expression froze for a second

too long to play it off as an accident, and she snatched up the napkin. The name 'Campion Merryweather' flashed on the screen.

"Back with him again, I see," I said humourlessly.

"Were you — did you take this? Were you reading my messages?"

"He's bad news, Holly," I growled, though I had lost all moral high ground when I cracked her password.

She squeezed her phone tightly between her fingers. "You're not my brother or my boyfriend, Sage, and even if you were either of those things, this is still a dick move. Keep your car, I know someone who can give me a lift." She stormed off, answering her phone as she went.

Me feeling guilty about reading her messages was not the reason that I felt like there was an industrial steel-capped cauldron weighing down the pit of my stomach.

———

IF I WAS STILL A SMOKER, the alley out the back of Cirque de Cacao would be a great place to hang out, but tonight it was cold and grey and sorta depressing. I stayed out there anyway, while the karaoke music started up inside.

Holly was right. I was being a dick. But the thought of Campion fucken Merryweather back in our lives, that put ice down the back of my neck.

Who was I to complain if she wanted to ditch the band? I was just the drummer.

"This is where you escaped to." Hebe came out of the coffee house like a breath of warm air, bringing my jacket with her. She shoved it in my general direction, because she is the best. "Did you have to tell Holly I have a crush on your new flatmate? Now she's trying to matchmake me through karaoke lyrics. It is the most horrifying thing I have ever experienced and I blame you."

I huffed out a laugh. "Could be worse."

She leaned her cheek on my shoulder, and my arm came

easily around her. "I don't have a crush on anyone," she muttered.

"Whatever you say, Hebes."

A buzz of magic burned through my skull. Some powerful workers were nearby, I could tell even through my caffeine haze. Powerful and angry. It tasted like the Real cafeteria in Finals Week, all fire and brimstone.

I slid my own phone — wrapped in cords and packed with salt so my skin never came into actual contact with it — and pulled up a familiar app.

"What's that?" Hebe asked curiously, then wrinkled her nose. "Do I even want to know?"

"Warlock'd," I said absently. "It's like Grindr but for magic users. Lets you find hookups who are power-compatible."

"Ew," she said, punching me lightly (but not that lightly) in the ribs. "Wait until you're not hugging your ex before you go trolling for talent."

"I'm not that tacky, darling, just trying to get a sense for who's around."

A blond face that I knew blew up on my screen. Jules Nightshade, arrogant Basilisk King prick who shared half my classes. Huh. His powers were mostly water and ice-based, which suited his personality down to the ground, and didn't account for the burning crackle in the back of my head.

The back door crashed open.

Hebe and I were snugged under the overhang, right in front of them, but the people who had just exploded out of the door didn't even see us. I glanced over and saw (rather than felt) that she was weaving her favourite spell, the 'don't notice' shield that Holly and I spent all of high school trying to convince her wasn't appropriate for every single social occasion.

Okay, this time it came in handy.

Jules Nightshade was practically dripping icicles and sarcasm all over the alleyway. The girl next to him was Viola Vale, a grad student from the Practical Mythology department, and there was that fire I'd been feeling in my head. Little sparks came off her fingernails and the ends of her eyelashes as she matched Nightshade for fury and cutting remarks.

In between them both was our Ferd — and yeah, he'd been living with me and Dec for less than a day but he was ours now, gotta protect your own. He was just as mad as his so called friends, but I didn't get a buzz of magic off him at all, not even a pale shadow.

Either he was really damned good at shielding his core, or… no, there was no or. According to his college record, he was top of his class in shadowmancy and had already been marked for a future career in Grey Ops. He was being mentored by Professor Hekate.

I'd only drunk one cappuccino. I should be able to sense something from him. What the hell was wrong with me?

"…just don't know what you're doing with these people," Viola hissed. "It's beneath you."

"While you're screwing around feeling sorry for yourself, we're trying to prevent you losing everything!" Jules growled.

"I already have lost everything!" Ferdinand yelled back at them both. The fire and ice of their magics rose and fell in an angry cloud around the three of them.

"We should go," whispered Hebe.

She was right — I'd invaded enough privacy for one day. With Hebe's 'don't notice' charm still wrapped around us, we slipped back into the coffee house just in time to hear one of my favourite songs of all time mangled by a first year Healing student who was high on sugar and marshmallows.

So that was Thursday.

CHAPTER 3

FRIDAY NIGHT SET LIST - REVISED! BY! HOLLY!

FIRST SET:

- Last Straight Girl in the City
- Coffee Shop AU With You
- Someone is Wrong on the Internet (Social Justice Warrior Remix)
- Time Agents Stole My Sister
- Bisexual Superhero Agenda
- Box Set Road Trip
- ~~Witches Roll Dice, Bitches~~

Sage says we can't have it as our finale every show, but who are we kidding?

[smoko]

SECOND SET:

- Put Me On Athena Owl's Roller Derby Team
- Stupid Songs About Victorian Novels

yes Juniper you have to sing it this time, it's amazing, shut up

- Manic Pixie Dream House
- Big Gay Break Up Song
- Witches Roll Dice, Bitches

MISCELLANEOUS:

- *??* So Real (So Unreal)

Sage says this isn't a Fake Geek Girl song. So what the hell is it?

- *???*

CHAPTER 4

THE ELEGANT AND ARTICULATE DIARY OF MISS JUNIPER CRESSWELL, GENTLEWITCH AND SCHOLAR.

SATURDAY

IT IS a truth universally acknowledged that a young lady of moderate intelligence who has an unhealthy adoration of Unreal Literature of the nineteenth century will inevitably end up writing a journal.

It is likewise inevitable that said journal should end up sounding somewhat like a pale imitation of Austen and Eliot, but hopefully nothing like Dickens, otherwise the young lady in question may have to put a wand to her head and hex her own brains all over the wall.

Let us be frank: there are other issues that the aforementioned young lady should probably be writing about, for the sake of working through her confused emotions, but probably shall not. These include:

A) *Holly Hallow and her pretty hair*
B) *belonging to a cult favourite band, thanks largely to her skills with the cello, triangle and assorted miscellaneous musical instruments*
C) *the young lady's own thighs and any conflicted feelings she may have about their size and*

>   *how they appear on stage with or without the*
>   *assistance of hoop skirts*
>   *D) Holly Hallow and her perfect body*
>   *E) Holly Hallow and her stupid boyfriend*
>   *F) the young lady having to hand-make her own*
>   *retro fashions rather than buying genuine*
>   *vintage because it's hard to find genuine*
>   *vintage above a size 16.*
>   *G) wanting to kiss stupid Holly Hallow*
>   *H) jogging*

Having established what this journal will not be about, and
something of its apparent signature style: Hello, my name is
Miss Juniper Cresswell. I am the lead cellist (which Sage assures
me is kind of like being the bass player) of a band called Fake
Geek Girl.

We're a bit famous, but I'm not being overly modest when I
add that qualification. It's difficult to quantify fame to any
degree, though apparently our fame is deserving of internet
cookies.

Trust me when I say that internet cookies are not a viable
currency in any economy, least of all an Australian university
campus where the College of the Real gets twice the funding and
attention as the College of the Unreal.

Last night, I sang a song in public.

This should be of no particular note, given that I am, as
previously mentioned, in a band, but this was different.

It was my song, and I sang it.

Fake Geek Girl has always been about Holly and her voice
and her writing - and also about Sage and his songs and his
ability to make magic happen, I don't mean the ordinary turning
people into frogs kind of magic, I mean knowing people and
arranging for things like a regular gig at Medea's Cauldron and
social media and making us go viral that one time. It's even
about Hebe, who isn't in the band but inspires most of the songs
one way or another.

It was about Nora too, but then she graduated and left the

band and the whole balance was off because it used to be a queer girl band that happened to have a male drummer, and then we were three and I never really felt like

I suspect I've lost my intended tone here.

I wrote "Stupid Songs About Victorian Novels" which is full of ideas from the thesis I haven't written yet, and my unrequited love for an indie rock queen, and my insecurity about being in a band that once went viral on YouTube (OMG) all wrapped up in a pretty lace bonnet. I never intended it to be a Fake Geek Girl song (because some songs just aren't) but Holly read it and she looked at me with those eyes of hers (SERIOUSLY THOSE EYES), and she insisted that I sing it, and she bought us parasols to open during the second verse, and she believed in me more than anyone has ever believed in me before.

Mostly it was the parasols. If I hadn't already gone stupid about her, I think that the parasols would have tipped me over the edge.

I've been getting up the nerve and losing it again for weeks, but last night I sang the song, and the audience cheered, and it was amazing. It was magic. It was the best night of my life.

Everything else is ghastly.

Holly and Sage are fighting, and that means not only that they're not talking to each other, which is awful, but little sparks of magic keep bouncing off them both and charging into the rest of us, so we're all about ready to kill each other.

I didn't want to come to Comfort Lunch. I always feel a bit on the outside anyway, because it's supposed to be a band thing but it's really more of a Manic Pixie Dream House thing, and I'm the only one now who boards over at the residential halls instead of living in the house.

We do it every Saturday, to wind down and regroup after the Friday night show. If we're in the downstairs flat then Holly cooks us something ridiculous and trendy out of a magazine, and if we're in the upstairs flat then Sage cooks something in the Carnivorous Crockpot of Doom.

It's nice except when Holly and Sage have their teeth into each other, and right now they're biting down hard. Nora used to

be amazing at calming them both, but she's gone and Hebe
won't pick sides. Mei buries herself in her laptop and her mirrors
and Dec talks about gaming and everyone pretends it's fine.

It's not fine.

It's not fine.

So today we were in the upstairs flat, and it was Ferd's first
introduction to this little tradition of ours. How is he supposed to
know it's not always this horrible?

We ate lasagne and garlic bread and chocolate cake, because
Sage is amazing in the kitchen when he is trying to rein in his
magic from setting fire to people, and the tension was so sharp I
could have plucked it like my cello strings.

The closest we came to a civilised conversation was this:

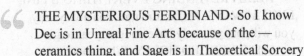

THE MYSTERIOUS FERDINAND: So I know
Dec is in Unreal Fine Arts because of the —
ceramics thing, and Sage is in Theoretical Sorcery
at the College of the Real, right?

ANGRY SNAPPY SAGE: Also Practical
Magery and Demonstrative Thaumaturgical
Phenomena. It's a triple major. I take night classes
in Unreal Engineering when I can, but they often
ban me if the equipment's too complex, because it
doesn't always stay in one piece when I'm
around.

THE MYSTERIOUS FERDINAND: That
seems… a lot.

DEC UNFLAPPABLE: He makes course counsellors cry.

THE MYSTERIOUS FERDINAND: So, uh,
what are the rest of you studying?

HEBE PRETENDING EVERYTHING'S FINE
LIKE ALWAYS: Unreal literature and gender
studies.

NERVOUS JITTERY MISS JUNIPER: We're
in some of the same literature classes! But my
major is political science.

MEI COOL AS A CUCUMBER: I'm doing a degree in Standard Magic.

ANGRY SNAPPY SAGE: Which is basically Generic Life Skills.

MEI COOL AS A CUCUMBER: It keeps my parents off my back, until I figure out how to make a living from fanfic.

DEC UNFLAPPABLE: No one ever makes a living from fanfic. That's not a thing.

MEI COOL AS A CUCUMBER: Brave new world, brave new business model.

SHARP-EDGED HOLLY: I do Real Arts/Law, but I'm thinking of dropping out.

HEBE PRETENDING EVERYTHING'S FINE LIKE ALWAYS: No, you're not. You always say you will, but you only have another year to go.

SHARP-EDGED HOLLY: What about you, Ferd of Mystery? Real, of course.

THE MYSTERIOUS FERDINAND: I'm, uh, thinking of making a change. I have a meeting with a course counsellor on Monday.

(Meaningful look between Ferd and Hebe. Goes on so long everyone feels kind of uncomfortable. Tension broken by Holly's phone chiming with a text message)

SHARP-EDGED HOLLY: Shall I read it out loud to you, Sage, or are you saving it for later?

ANGRY SNAPPY SAGE: Give it a fucking rest, will you?

After the chilly, awkward silence that followed, Dec started to explain this vintage tabletop game he had just bought. Ferd knew an out when he saw it, and pretended to be ever so interested, then Hebe threw herself at both of them, claiming to be desperate to teach Ferd about dice rules.

For one horrible moment I realised they were doing it to

leave the band alone together, then I remembered that I was an adult and could pretend to be interested in gaming if I wanted.

So the rest of us ended up in Dec's room playing a game about retro magical artefacts while Holly and Sage spat magical sparks of passive aggressiveness at each other in the kitchen. I sat on Dec's bed with Mei and we watched Hebe and Ferb struggled to perform a subtle and restrained kind of flirting that even I left behind at high school.

Mei ran her finger lightly over the mirror that lay on her lap, and the words

> I DUB THEM HEEBPHOENIX, AND I SHALL SHIP THEM FOREVER

appeared in magical smoke on the glass.

I touched my own finger to the mirror:

> ONE TRUE PAIRING

Mei smiled, which isn't something she generally does in my presence.

So it wasn't a completely ghastly day after all.

Ghastly didn't happen until 4am the next morning.

CHAPTER 5
HEBE & THE MAGICAL FIRE ALARM MEET-CUTE

SUNDAY

I HAD no idea why Sage and Holly were fighting. Something to do with the band.

They'd fought about me once, long ago, around the time of the Most Chill Breakup Ever Told and I'd made them swear that they would never do that again. So usually when their tempers spark up, it's a creative differences thing.

I knew I should have banged their heads together yesterday after the disastrously uncomfortable Comfort Lunch, but hiding meant spending time with Phoenix Boy AKA Ferdinand.

I was weak. I chose a cute boy over making peace between my sister and my… Sage.

I should have known that meant I was also choosing a cute boy over a good night's sleep.

Our fire alarm + volatile emotions = a recipe for disaster.

The Manic Pixie Dream House contains six people of varying degrees of magic from mine (mild, inoffensive) to Holly's (volatile and dramatic) all the way to Sage's (may someday be weaponised by our government).

Add to that the various people who sleep over: Mei's ex-girlfriend, Sage's various hookups (he tends to be drawn to men with powers as ridiculously overloaded as his own, which I used to think was a weird coincidence until I found out he had an app for that, OMG), Holly's terrible temporary partners (her last boyfriend was so vile that Mei and I invented a new language to talk about him behind his back), Juniper on the nights she crashes on our couch, Nora when she's visiting, etc.

We take all the precautions that we can: we wrap and charm our modern tech so it doesn't glitch too much against the magical vibes, we use enchanted alternatives, and yes, those of us whose magic isn't vital to our sense of identity do sometimes drink a cup of coffee to drown it all out.

But still.

Rental properties in Australia legally require a dual fire alarm system: magical and technological. These are traditionally unreliable as is any system combining magic and technology. Added to that, we have Sage, who can't leave any system alone, and has a tendency to add his own — let's say improvements.

Oh, the thing detects smoke okay. And fire. But it also gets oversensitive about turbulent magical vibrations, or if there's a build up of fire or air magic in the atmosphere, or if two or three high-powered magic users are having a bad night's sleep at the same time.

Once, on a supremely embarrassing occasion, we're pretty sure it reacted to the fact that energetic sex was happening in four of the six bedrooms in the house.

This time, I felt it early, a deep shiver of a warning that filled my room with a warm green light. Pink sparkles in my mouth. There's only one thing in the world that tastes like pink sparkles.

"FIRE ALARM!" I yelled and scrambled up, out of bed, stopping only briefly to check that I was wearing nice pyjamas that weren't completely gross (because there's survival instincts, and then there's the possibility of being embarrassed in front of that boy you like) before I cannonballed out of my bedroom.

I met Mei on my way out, carrying her emergency padded bag full of laptops and her other emergency padded bag full of mirrors. She stopped to shake Juniper (who had crashed on our couch last night) while I woke up my sister, who sat up with her long hair bursting around her scalp like a dandelion cloud of static electricity.

"I'm going to kill him," Holly hissed like a snake, and charged out of the flat, dressed only in a pair of Belladonna Bunyips boxer shorts and a too-small Bromancers t-shirt she had stolen from me because she liked the design.

We made it outside before the first intense sweep, which is designed to seek unintended heat sources and snuff them out, but to humans feels like a magical skin peel.

Dec and Sage burst out of the back door a few minutes after us, gasping and shaking because they'd been caught in the tail end of the sweep. Ick. I tried to sleep through the damn thing once, and it felt like someone had transformed my back teeth into shattered barley sugars.

"Where's Ferd?" I yelled at them, because they had apparently abandoned their new roommate to the inhumane terrors of the fire alarm (which was now bathing every room in a piercing blue light that comes with a fun anti-flame steam so hot that it makes anyone with magical senses want to claw their own face off).

Ferdinand Chauvelin walked calmly out of the house in a beautiful satin dressing gown, as if nothing very exciting was happening.

It was at that point that I suspected he wasn't actually human.

"Don't worry about it, mate," said Sage, picking himself up off the grass. "Only another ten minutes and we can go back inside."

"If you say so," said Ferd, yawning.

"Being stuck outside for a fire alarm is a surprisingly popular theme for fanfic meet-cutes," said Mei out of nowhere. "It's not up there in popularity with coffee shop AUs or non magical boarding schools, but it's gaining traction as a trope."

"Ugh," said Holly.

It started to rain.

"UGH," said Holly, and this time it was directed straight at Sage.

Ferd came over next to me and opened an umbrella. "I thought we might need this."

I smiled sweetly and managed not to say "How are you so perfect?" because that would have just been embarrassing.

We stood there in the rain, watching our house explode into a rainbow variety of colours, while it made absolutely certain that nothing was on fire.

"Ironically," said Dec. "That one time when we actually did set the stove on fire, it didn't make a peep."

"I always feel so safe when I stay here," Juniper sighed.

———

LATER, when Mei was towelling off her hair before we all went back to bed, she asked me, "Have you spotted it yet?"

"Spotted what?" I asked defensively.

"*Any* imperfection that will allow you to treat Ferd like he's a human being instead of some weird godlike creature you put on a shelf and stare at from very far away."

"Don't — that just makes me sound creepy!" I wailed.

Mei could be relentless when rain-soaked and annoyed. "We're all shipping the two of you, but if it takes much longer we're all going to get bored and start slashing him with Dec instead."

I stared at her, open-mouthed. "Dec's straight. Why wouldn't you slash him with Sage?"

"Slashing him with an actual gay bloke is no fun at all. It's practically cheating."

Holly huffed impatiently. "I don't know what you're talking about, because I thought shipping and slashing was the same thing, but I don't care. There's a pretty obvious imperfection if you're looking for one."

"I'm not," I said automatically. "But, um. What?"

"Isn't it obvious? He doesn't respond to magic at all. He's a null."

CHAPTER 6

TEXTS FROM MONDAY!!!

HOLLY: Where are you???

HOLLY: Come on, this isn't fair, you don't ditch practice just because we're fighting

HOLLY: You're a dickhead

HOLLY: Since when do you care who I date, anyway? You never like any of my boyfriends or girlfriends.

SAGE: That's because you have shit taste in people

HOLLY: He lives!

SAGE: Look you want to hang out with a wanker who treated you like crap the last two times you were together, whatever. I don't care about Campion fucking Merryweather

SAGE: You know he's using you.

HOLLY: Is this about his Dad?

HOLLY: So his Dad owns a record label, how exactly does that mean Campion's using me? MantiCore don't give a rat's arse about Fake Geek Girl, if that's what's pissing in your beer

SAGE: I know they don't.

HOLLY: ???

HOLLY: ???????

HOLLY: U suck

CHAPTER 7

SAGE'S COFFEE SHOP AU

TUESDAY

BACK AT CIRQUE DE CACAO, because half the people I live with were pissed off at me, and the other half were busy with their own melodrama.

I chugged two mochaccinos down in under half an hour. If I didn't quiet the random magical blasts from my skin, I was gonna have to find another coffee shop because this one would be a charred mess of foamed milk and hipsters.

Then, because I was good for nothing else this week, I devoted my attention to scribbling down angry song lyrics on a stack of circus-themed serviettes.

"I'm the last straight girl in this city,
    But I'm changing my mind, oh I'm changing my mind.
    I'm the last straight girl in this city,
    But I'm changing my mind because
    YOU'RE SO PRETTY!"

I glared at the sound system and then at Skinny Goth Waiter who is usually better than this. "Did you do that deliberately?"

"You looked like you needed cheering up," he said in a deadpan voice.

Yeah, right. I gave him a filthy look. "You friends with Holly or Juniper?"

Skinny Goth Waiter smiled with all his teeth. "Juniper wanted me to punish you for skipping band practice. She said I could get creative with my methods. By the way, someone tweeted your location and there's a bunch of thirteen year old fans outside who want your autograph."

I'm pretty sure I had a haunted look on my face as I looked up at the picture windows.

Skinny Goth Waiter just about killed himself laughing. "I'm kidding," he said. "But that was great. Can I get a selfie with you?"

"Sure, just let me stick this fork in my neck real quick." But I let him take the picture and even put a deliberately suffering expression on my face while I did it.

On another day, I would have appreciated his trolling tactics for the minor work of art that they were.

He didn't let up on the sound system, so I wrote my angry This Is How The Band Breaks Up song to the background melody of Fake Geek Girl's greatest hits.

Magic is a huge force in our lives. Even people who don't have much of it — I reckon their lives revolve around it even more. My parents obsessed over how to keep it out of our world. These days, now I know how much power I have bubbling under my skin and how dangerous it might be if I let it loose — I can *never* not think about it.

Even if I wasn't such a freak of nature, I'd still be the sort of bloke who spends all his time trying to figure out how everything works, from the inside out, and magic is a big part of that.

It's not an original thought. Hell, pretty much every student at the College of the Real is trying to figure out how magic works, from first principles.

But give me a band. A band — a good band, one that really speaks to people — is a perfect combo of instruments, performers, fans, lyrics, beat, heart. It's all set list and history and atmosphere and singing yourself raw on a Friday night.

No one's ever going to write a thesis on how that kinda magic happens. But it is magic, it's the best kind of magic, and it only works when all the ingredients are in sync with each other. Take one thing away, and maybe you can recover. Take two things, and it's broken.

I wrote, and I drank coffee until Skinny Goth Waiter cut me off and asked pointed questions about when I last ate anything, and I wrote more, and while that was happening my phone blew up with more messages — not from Holly this time, she'd given up on me after yesterday — but Juniper, mostly, harassing me about skipping practice in her perfectly grammatical texts.

Dec, too, because I'd blown off a mirror raid I promised to play with him yesterday. I was letting everyone down, I knew it.

I've never been real good at letting go of stuff, and I didn't know how to let go of this. I didn't know how to come to terms with Fake Geek Girl being that thing we did one time before our lives got started.

When I was done, I had three songs, and they were all written for Holly's voice, and Juniper's cello.

We were so screwed.

I blinked when a plate full of grilled sandwich and hot chips appeared in front of me, like a mirage. Hebe sat across from the table, with that little frown line between her eyebrows she gets when she's worried. "Will said you looked like you were about to keel over," she said.

"Who the fuck's Will?"

She pointed to Skinny Goth Waiter who gave me an embarrassed sort of salute.

"Huh." I started to eat the sandwich and discovered after about three bites that yeah, I was hungry.

"What's going on with you, Sage?" Hebe asked softly.

And this was it, right? The point where I unloaded all my bullshit and she fixed it somehow, or at least helped me come to terms with what couldn't be fixed. That's how it usually goes.

Me and Hebe, fixing things.

But she had a look on her face that was maybe not about me, and it felt all of a sudden like I'd spent so much time this week being pissed off at her mirror image that we'd hardly seen each other.

"You first," I said, and went back to attacking my sandwich.

Hebe bit on her lower lip. "Well…" she said uncertainly.

It all came tumbling out. How she was pretty sure — at least, Holly had put it together — that Ferd was a null, which made no sense, not for a third year Basilisk King, but if you put it together with the Thaumaturgy explosion last year, and the rumours, and the…

I had my own side to add at that point, because it was pretty damned obvious in the alley last week when his friends were all powered up and I couldn't feel a spark from him, and then again on the night of the fire alarm when he walked through the wave without a peep. But I'd been too wrapped up in my own head to pay attention.

"His tattoo still moves," I said thoughtfully.

"That's not him, though, is it? Magical tattoos are — well. They have their own sources of power."

I couldn't imagine it. Moving through our world without any magic at all, that would be hard. I spent the first seventeen years of my life being pressured to avoid, ignore, do without it, but it was still there in the air around me.

Going from that, though, from full-blown legacy student of the Real with so much family expectation to… nothing. How did a Basilisk King cope with that?

"I guess," I said thoughtfully, wiping up sauce with my chips. "If he's lucky, he'll find a cool place to live, and a bunch of new friends who won't be all judgy and weird about it. He could flirt with a girl who doesn't see him as a stepping stone to the wealth and privilege of the Founders. He could enrol in some courses at that College of the Unreal I hear so much about. Maybe even pick up a few non-magical life skills along the way. And — I feel that an introduction to tabletop games and the wonders of the internet would help round out his experience of being among the Unreal peasants."

Hebe gave me the most ridiculous grin. It was a good look on her. "Sage," she said fondly. "Are you suggesting that there's nothing to be fixed here?"

"Take it as a win, darling."

That, right there. That was a quit while you're ahead kind of moment. I should have finished my chips, sent Hebe on her way to take things up a notch with the sizzling Ferdinand, and wandered over to see if Skinny Goth Waiter wanted to give me his number.

Instead, when Hebe looked serious and said "Now it's your turn," I told her the truth.

I told her that I was pretty sure Holly was going to break up with the band, to leave all the geeky in jokes and internet fame behind in exchange for a more normal solo career.

And Hebe thought about it for about thirty seconds, then replied: "Well, maybe she should."

———

WE WERE STILL YELLING at each other when we got back to the house.

CHAPTER 8
HURT/COMFORT AND HOLLY

WEDNESDAY

Hey Noracakes

I know it's been forever, and you're busy ~~selling out living a directionless and uncreative life~~ working, but I wanted to check in.

Big question, and no one around here is up for giving me an unbiased answer, so I thought

Obviously I can ask Hebe because I can tell Hebe anything, but she's so damned perfect and all our friends are really her friends, and how did that even happen?

~~I'm pretty sure I used to be the popular one.~~

Thing is, when I came back to the house yesterday because I was all weirded out by this lunch I'd had with Campion (yes, Campion and I are back together, he's really grown as a person and no, no he hasn't I have no excuse) the first thing I heard was Hebe and Sage going at it, really fighting, and you know they never fight, they didn't even fight when they broke up, though it might have been better if they did...

Back to today. Hebe yelled "__for the last time, Holly is not my FAULT__" and they slammed doors at each other, and I don't even think either of them knew I was home.

~~It wasn't meant to be cruel or anything~~

But

So I had a question to ask you. How do you know when it's time to stop?

I mean, it was easier for you I guess because you graduated, and that's like finishing high school when you realise something huge in your life is coming to an end, so maybe it's a good time to finally break up with your latest terrible boyfriend, or start a band with your sister's ex because he's one of your favourite people in the world and you don't want him to disappear from your life.

But let's say you didn't graduate last year. Was it still the right time for you to quit the band? What if there aren't any major milestones coming up, but maybe it's still time to

Campion thinks I should go solo, that maybe I've gone as far as I can with Fake Geek Girl.

He's a dick, I know he's a dick, and I really need to break up with him again

(but that doesn't mean he's wrong)

Maybe I've gone further than I ever meant to with a band that advertises to the world that I have no idea what I'm doing

I just

This is the stupidest email I have ever written. ~~I can't even~~

You were always really good at taking the stupid shit that I wrote and making it amazing. Maybe we should have called it a day when you left

Juniper misses you heaps.

I

You are still the most cool person I know and singing Someone is Wrong on the Internet without you is so beyond weird that we've got a new arrangement now just to keep it making sense to us, and any time, literally any time you are passing Hemlock Square on a Friday night (or maybe a Thursday for Karaoke we're not proud) come see us

Love

Hollyrageous xxxxx

CHAPTER 9

A GENTLEWITCH'S GUIDE TO SAVING THE WORLD, BY MISS JUNIPER CRESSWELL, ESQUIRE.

THURSDAY

- Step 1: Bond with a certain Mr Ferdinand Chauvelin over the many ways in which we are now disappointing our families, and also our mutual admiration for the Hallow sisters.
- Step 2: Pause to unravel the amusing misunderstanding that we might in fact be romantically interested in the same Hallow sister. Thank goodness we're not! Moving on.
- Step 3: Talk to Sage to find out exactly what happened
- Step 4: Smack Sage around his over-muscled shoulders several times because he's a self-destructive moron.
- Step 5: Talk to Hebe
- Step 6: Talk to Holly
- Step 7: Reconvene with Mr Ferdinand Chauvelin to lament how terrible Sage, Hebe and Holly are at using THEIR WORDS when it comes to things that FREAKING MATTER.
- Step 8: Tea and biscuits

- Step 9: Agree to an over-elaborate plan which involves Ferdinand and myself luring Holly and Hebe separately to the Desiree O'Dowd Unreal Library on Thursday evening, and locking them both in the highly unhexable resources cabinet so that they can talk about their problems without interruption.

- Step 10: Arrange for Sage to collect them from their impromptu prison at midnight without telling him that this is so that the three of them can in fact have a sensible conversation about NOT BREAKING UP THE BAND GODDAMN IT.

- Step 11: While awaiting the results, discover that Mr Ferdinand Chauvelin is entirely unaware of *First Impressions*, the BBC TV series from the late 90's in which the story of Pride and Prejudice is retold as a non-magical alternate universe, featuring Julia Sawahla and Rupert Graves. Squee!

- Step 12: Kick Dec out of his own flat so that Ferd and I can watch the DVD box set of *First Impressions* uninterrupted for several hours. With cake.

- Step 13. More cake.

CHAPTER 10

HEBE AND THE LIBRARY RESOURCE CUPBOARD OF DOOM.

FRIDAY [ABOUT A MINUTE AFTER MIDNIGHT ON A THURSDAY NIGHT, THAT COUNTS AS FRIDAY, RIGHT?]

THE KEY TURNED in the lock, finally, and Sage stood there to release us — a sheepish, guilty-looking Sage. "Before you start, this wasn't my idea," he said. "I think we might actually have broken Juniper…"

"Not yet," I said, and slammed the door of the resource cupboard shut in his face, turning back to my sister. "We're not finished."

"You realise you live together, right?" Sage said through the door. "You have a really comfy couch at home, and also snacks."

I ignored him, and leaned against the door. "Say it again."

"You're my sister and I love you," sighed Holly.

"Not that part. I know that part."

Holly took a deep breath and met my eyes, looking at me with a bleak expression. I don't know how people struggle to tell us apart. My face is nothing like her face. "You and Sage have been falling over yourselves to tell me that I want a solo career, that I was always going to grow out of fronting a band that's all about your nerd stuff."

I stared at her, because we had been circling this for hours, ever since Juniper and Ferd pulled their trick on us. We had, admittedly, spent an awful lot of the Resource Cupboard Discussion Time going over issues to do with Holly's renewed relationship with Campion Merryweather, and why she had felt the need to hide it from me, and yes she was TOTALLY breaking up with him this week because OMG he was bad for her.

But the band stuff — this was material we'd never actually gone into, not the two of us. It was amazing how you could live with someone, share a family and a house with them, and spend so little time talking about what matters.

"We just assumed," I said desperately, and hoped Sage was listening, because this was for him too.

"You thought I was too shallow to write songs about things I actually care about," Holly protested. "Like, I must have had nothing better to write songs about, so why not your shit?"

"I didn't say that!"

"Did it ever occur to you that I spend so much time writing and singing about things you love because —" and she paused there, running out of steam. "Oh, I don't know."

"Don't stop there," I whispered.

"Can I come in yet?" Sage asked through the door.

"No!" we both snapped at him.

Holly twisted her mouth at me. "You and Sage and Juniper and Mei and Dec and Nora — you care about the things you love so much. It doesn't always make sense to me — you really don't make sense to me like half the time, it's ridiculous — but it's interesting. It's worth singing about. I've never loved anything as much as you love your fictional characters and their imaginary relationships and that secret language that you all speak —"

"It's not a secret language, it's just how people communicate on the internet."

"WHATEVER." She threw up her hands. "Do you remember the first song we did? Me and Sage, before we found Nora and Juniper and made it a real band?"

I started smiling, because I did remember. "Time Agents Stole My Sister."

"High school was nearly over and we saw less and less of each other. I read *Athena Owl*, all fourteen volumes of that stupid bloody manga, because I was sick of not being able to talk to you about anything anymore, and I hated it."

I laughed. "You pretended to like it."

"I. Hated. It. I wrote the song because I was genuinely pissed off but then Sage helped me with it and somehow it turned out funny and you thought it was good."

"It was great. It's still my favourite. I didn't even know you knew half the in jokes you reference in that song."

Holly gave me a sideways grin. "I didn't. I still don't."

"Liar."

She shrugged. "I suppose I've picked up a few things over the years… and I do like the queer subtext in all your dumb shows."

"Sometimes it's not even subtext. Sometimes it's just text."

"Yeah, but those two dudes in *The Bromancers* are never going to get together, Hebes. Never ever."

"Is there hugging yet?" Sage said pitifully through the door. "Can we skip to the hugging."

"Nearly," called Holly, and then she hugged me just to spite him. "Thing is, I started Fake Geek Girl, and I stuck with it, because I love the way you love things. The way you look at the world. It's weird, but it's interesting. I've never felt that passionately about anything but music, and I don't want to make a career of writing songs about being a musician, that's one step away from circling the drain."

Sage did open the door, then. He looked, if possible, about twice as pitiful as the first time he did it. "So you're not ditching Fake Geek Girl to run off and sing songs about — I don't know, love and breakups and boring shit like that?"

Holly rolled her eyes at him as she hugged me again. "Sage, Fake Geek Girl is *my band*. If you try to take it off me, I'm going to go after you with that replica dwarven axe Hebe keeps under the bed."

"Also," I said, pushing Holly's hair out of my face. "All your songs are about love and breakups already. Or hadn't you noticed?"

Holly and Sage looked at each other and did their silent apology thing.

"Come on," said Holly. "I need to write a song about how dumb you both are. Let's go home."

CHAPTER 11

GENERIC LOVE SONG (SOMETHING ABOUT SPOILERS)

BY FAKE GEEK GIRL

I love you so much that I care your favourite show got cancelled
> *Again*
> *I care that they whitewashed the casting,*
> *And queerbaited the fans*
> *And they fridged three female lead characters*
one after the other
> *That really sucks*
> *I'm so sorry*
> *And something about spoilers*

I love that you care that your game just isn't the same without mirrors
> *I love that you care that two fictional characters who never kiss on the mouth might someday get married*
> *Or have a threesome*
> *With that one guy whose name I can never remember*
> *But he's totally in that other show that you love*
> *Not the one that got cancelled*
> *The other one*
> *This is how much I love you*

This is how much I care
I don't understand why you have to see the
movie the first day it comes out even though the
line's super long and it will be the exact same
movie if you see it a week later
Because something about spoilers

I love you
And that's why I care
That the award went to the wrong writer
In fact all the awards are broken
And the reviewers are sexist
And you and your best friend are fighting
The best friend I've never met
Because she lives on the internet
And something about spoilers

I don't really care
But I love that you care
I love that you have a whole secret language of
letters
OMG OTP OT3 WTF it all means something
to you
Actually I'm pretty clear on WTF
We have that one in the real world too
I love you so much that I read a book with
vampires in it
Even though they made a TV show about it and
I could watch that instead
The book was quite terrible
But I'm reading the sequel
I won't ever tell you
Because I love that expression on your face
When I say I'm going to look up the ending on
Wikipedia
I don't care about spoilers
But you really do

I love you
    I love your thirty five fandoms
    And your one true pairings
    And your intense flamewars about pop culture
analysis
    And your games with imaginary friends
    And the way you watch TV shows like someone
is scoring points
    (and maybe someday you'll win)
    I love all these things about you
    I don't really care
    But I love that you care
    And something about spoilers

UNMAGICAL BOY STORY

PART ONE

MONDAY MORNING

CHAPTER 1

9AM, FAR TOO EARLY

THE LECTURE HALL is full of buzz and roar — conference delegates from every Magical Theory department in the country, and a few international guests. Grad students, of course, dozens of them, all nursing their own papers to be presented at some point over the next three days. Having this many magical adepts in the same space means a tension in the air that can't be fully compensated for by the hex-dampeners built into the walls.

Coffee helps. At gatherings like this, coffee is the most effective dampener of magic. Those to-go cups clutched in the fists of the professors and grad students alike reduce the risk of an academic debate turning into a literal tornado of static and feelings.

Viola didn't get up early enough to grab a coffee, and she regrets that now. Why does she have to be the first speaker?

Why does she have to do this at all? Couldn't she just have ditched university after her first degree and signed up to be someone's trophy wife, like her father always wanted?

It's not too late. She could trophy wife the hell out of someone. Right now, that seems a better bet than the cool, crisp pages beneath her fingers, and the knowledge that she would have more time to perfect her paper it if she hadn't spent the entire weekend recovering from Friday night.

It's all Chauvelin's fault. It's all Jules Nightshade's fault. It's the fault of that inane band that everyone loves so much.

This is all her own fault.

Professor Medeous finishes a passive-aggressive conversation with Professor Hekate, then rises to make the introduction. "First we shall hear from one of the more promising doctoral students specialising in Practical Mythology here at Belladonna University, current holder of the Pandemonium Prize for Innovation: Ms Viola Vale."

Viola steps forward: a small half-Chinese woman, 20 years old, poised and elegant with a black bob of hair and a gleam of pearls at her throat, her silk cheongsam barely visible beneath the academic gown.

Her voice, when she speaks, is calm and precise, despite the whirl of nerves and magical flame under her skin. "I am told that by the second year of postgrad, most students are ready to set their exegesis — or their supervisor — on fire. I thought I'd save time and energy by concentrating my efforts on the myth of Prometheus."

She pauses for the small ripple of laughter, here and there among the deep tiers of seats. "Those of you in the audience who laughed at that, you're my favourites."

Then she pauses, caught off guard, by a familiar face in the back row. Not him, not here. She wasn't expecting...

The show must go on, of course.

She speaks: "The earliest versions of the Prometheus story come to us from Hesiod, both in the *Theogony* and his later poem, *Works and Days*. Everyone knows that Prometheus stole fire from the gods, but the part of the story that is less well known is that Zeus stole it first. He took fire — our own innovation — away from humanity as a punishment. When we suffered for lack of fire, Prometheus stole it back, on our behalf. Zeus further retaliated by creating Pandora, or "all gifts," a woman who carried a jar full of great evils, and was so curious that she unleashed them on the world."

Viola pauses for effect, tugging her robe straight, and refusing to look up, up at the back row. *I'm sorry. I swear, I didn't mean this to get so personal.* Something inside her has shifted and changed, and that couldn't help but be reflected in the paper that she wrote and rewrote and tweaked.

After Friday night.

Suck it up, Vale.

"It's a good story," she says, her voice ringing clearly across the lecture hall. "But like many of our ancient sources, Hesiod doesn't begin to make sense until you accept the premise that he was speaking in metaphor. 'Fire' does not mean actual fire any more than the jar was a literal jar. If you read the *Theogony* as a treatise on the Real and the Unreal, our society split as it always has been into two halves, then the Prometheus myth is clearly about human society's reliance on magic, and our collective fear that one day, the gods will take it back."

PART TWO

FRIDAY NIGHT

CHAPTER 2

7PM, LITTLE BLACK DRESS ALERT

VIOLA VALE KNEW she was in trouble when she peered at her tired, un-made up face in the bathroom mirror, and it flashed the words 'little black dress alert' in poison green.

Oh, hell no.

"No," she ordered the mirror, and watched the word appear in her own signature purple font before she turned around, and returned to bed.

Viola's bed was covered with her essential texts, a roll of parchment, and an Unreal laptop sealed in a containment bubble to protect it from the magic that infused her room.

So many stressed out, over-achieving Real Witch postgrads had occupied this room over the decades — a plum piece of residential hall real estate, a corner single with a view of the Belladonna U quad and easy fire escape access to one of the best magical libraries on campus. Electronics never lasted long around here. The walls practically vibrated with mood altering enchantments.

As Viola attempted to sink herself back into her analysis of Hesiod, the small hand mirror beside her bed blinked the words, 'little black dress alert.'

"Goblindamnit." How many mirrors did she have, anyway? Too bloody many.

Head down, Viola immersed herself in medieval interpretations of the Prometheus myth, making careful notes as she went. She had ten minutes of peace before frost cracked a pattern against her window, with the words 'little black dress alert' written on the fogged glass.

The temperature had dropped about ten degrees, and if she used her own magic to warm herself up, she risked setting fire to the doona cover. Again.

Viola dropped her quill and stormed over to fling open the window. "WORLD OF NO, NIGHTSHADE," she howled into the now-chilly evening.

A beautiful blond incubus of a man slid in through the gap before she could pull the window closed. Jules Nightshade. He lounged against her bookcase as if he belonged here, all skinny leather trousers, moon-pale skin and pixie-sparkle hair product.

"You know you want to," he drawled at her.

"I have a paper to present at the Conference of Mystical Confluence first thing on Monday morning, Jules," Viola said snappishly. "I don't have time for your usual weekend riot of clubbing and shenanigans."

"No one does homework on a Friday night, Vale," said her best friend in the world. "You'll grow old before your time."

"This isn't homework, it's real work. This conference is a chance to make an impression on..." Viola trailed off, because Jules didn't care about professional reputation, or her future in academia. Like her, he had grown up in a world where Daddy bought you anything you wanted.

It took Viola a long time to learn that the things Daddy couldn't buy for her were the only things worth having, and even longer to learn that Jules would never join her on that ride.

"I have to work all weekend to get this perfect," she said finally. "It's important."

Jules rolled his eyes. "You don't have to work at anything, Vale. You snap your fingers and the world bends to your will."

"Fuck *you*," she said, because he really didn't get it. Bad enough that everyone in the world saw that when they looked at her — the spoiled princess who got everything without even trying. There had always been two people she relied on to know who she truly was underneath the bitchery and rose-scented lip gloss. Jules Nightshade was one of them.

The other was gone, and his absence still burned like iron on a hexed tattoo.

Jules didn't realise that he had said something unforgivable. "You need a relaxing night out, honeybunch."

"I am not going to to blow off a chance to look brilliant in front of every magical theorist I respect in this country. Especially not to spend a crappy night downing cheap mojitos while you hit on every twink in sight and pretend you're not nursing a massive crush on six foot of indie drummer."

Jules didn't react to her low blow, which was in retrospect something of a warning sign. He batted his eyelashes. "Chauvelin invited us."

Oh. Viola felt a jolt of flames in her stomach. "You talked to him?"

Jules shifted uncomfortably, which was out of character. He usually had no shame. Perhaps his trousers were too tight for his ego. "You know he's seeing that girl?"

"The one from the terrible band with the drummer you don't have a crush on?"

"No, actually. Her sister. But yes, that band, shut up. Chauv and his new girlfriend go every Friday to watch the band, and he asked us along."

This was huge. Ever since the accident, since everything changed, there had been little contact between Viola and Jules and their other best friend. Ferdinand Chauvelin, who wasn't one of them any more.

Who had spent the whole summer and half of first semester pretending that he wasn't a Basilisk King, that he didn't share their history. They'd fought with him about it — each argument more explosive and messy and cruel than the last — but they hadn't exactly talked. Without Chauv to balance them on an everyday basis, Jules and Viola had sharpened themselves on each other like edged weapons.

It hurt that Chauvelin had shut them out. It hurt worse that, deprived of his steady influence, they became awful human beings.

"He invited us," she repeated.

"One drink?" Jules purred. "One drink, mend the rift, best of friends again, early night, work on your paper thing tomorrow?"

Oh hell. Time to dig out a little black dress.

"One drink," Viola warned. "Early night. Work tomorrow."

Jules looked far too pleased with himself. Viola could tell already that this was a terrible mistake.

She made it anyway.

Sometimes you just have to leap off a cliff, and hope someone hands you a hex-free cocktail on the way down.

CHAPTER 3

8PM, COVER CHARGE: TWO DRINKS

MEDEA'S CAULDRON had a two drinks cover charge on a Friday night. Because of course they did.

"Do you think they'll waive the requirement for me if I tell them how much I hate the band?" Viola asked as she and Jules made their way to the table.

Who was she kidding? One vodka elderberry wasn't going to cut it. Not for this. *This* being, as it turned out, the most awkward double date in the history of everything.

"I'm glad you came," said Ferdinand Chauvelin, looking relaxed and happy and beautiful. His black hair was buzzed closer than usual, so it didn't curl. He still dressed like himself — a quality white silk shirt, unbuttoned enough to show off the endlessly burning wing of his phoenix tattoo against the deep brown of his skin.

He wasn't wearing his usual amulets. Not even the bronze knot of protection that Viola gave him for his eighteenth birthday.

"Of course," she said, and took his hand in a squeeze, because she wasn't a total bitch. "It's good to see you, Chauv."

That was a lie. It was awful to see him so damned comfortable in a grungy crowded pub, instead of lurking in a more elegant establishment with his real friends, being snarky and hilarious.

"This is Hebe Hallow," Chauvelin added, with hearts in his eyes.

The mousy girl beside him gave Jules and Viola a wary nod. She wasn't a pushover, then. She wasn't unmagical, either. Her skin tingled against Viola's as they clasped hands in the traditional friendly (not too friendly) greeting. There was nothing extraordinary about this girl, but the Hallows were an old and respectable family.

He could have done worse. When Viola first heard that Chauv had transferred to the College of the Unreal and was dating a girl from the other side of Hemlock Square, she had imagined him slumming it with a null or a newbie.

Realisation crashed in on her all over again that Chauvelin, *her Chauvelin*, was a null himself. Maybe forever. How did you survive without magic in this world?

Jules took over the conversation, chatting to Hebe Hallow about the band, and her studies, like he was the tolerant and supportive friend of the group — like he hadn't broken three mirrors when he first heard Chauv transferred out of the College of the Real without even talking to them about it.

Good Witch, Bad Witch, was that how they were playing this? How long could Jules keep up the pretense that he was the nice one?

"How is it on the other side of campus?" Viola broke in, gaze fixed on Chauvelin, as if there was no one else in the noisy pub. "Are they starting you off in kindergarten, or do you get to count your lost magical years towards some kind of qualification?"

Hebe flinched at Viola's sharp tone. Chauvelin took it in his stride. "My degree will be mixed," he said. "That's allowed, these days. I've completed enough shadowmancy units already to count that as a major, but I'm trying a bunch of different Unreal subjects right now. No point in specialising until I know what I like."

"You were supposed to graduate at the end of this year," Viola said, stabbing her vodka elderberry with a straw.

"Now I probably won't," said Chauvelin, his voice going darker, in a warning tone. "It's not the end of the world."

"You realise you could have taken a year of theory classes with us and completed a Real Degree by November."

"Of course I realise," he snapped. "We don't all enjoy reading about other people performing magic, Vale. What's the point of graduating with a Real degree I can never use?"

Heat sizzled under her fingertips. If she didn't let her anger out properly, she was likely to set fire to the table. "I suppose I would have known you felt that way. If you had talked to us at all in the last few months."

A flash of guilt crossed Chauvelin's face, but then Hebe Hallow covered his hand with her own, and the guilt vanished.

Viola knocked back the last of her drink. "Look at that. I need a second one after all."

———

JULES CAUGHT up with her at the bar. "Quite a show, precious. Tell us what you really feel."

Viola's whole body trembled with rage. She didn't do this, didn't let feelings get to her, not in grubby little dive bars where the bartender — *hello* — wouldn't even make eye contact with her, too busy pouring cocktails for a bunch of Fake Geek Girl fans in homemade t-shirts.

"You did this deliberately," she said bitterly.

"Vale…" Jules drawled. Which wasn't an answer.

"I'm impressed. It was a tidy piece of strategy. Let me bitch out, so you don't have to play the villain."

Jules bumped his hips against hers. "It worked, didn't it? At least he'll be texting one of us next time he makes a major life change."

"I am not a wand," Viola spat. "Don't point me at your enemies."

Hurt flared in his eyes, and an icicle began to form beneath the bar where Jules was resting his hand. "Chauv isn't our enemy."

Viola finally caught the eye of the bartender, who came over to mix her a new drink. "I hate to break it to you, *precious*, but I don't think he's a friend any more."

————

JULES NIGHTSHADE HAD ALWAYS BEEN a little shit.

They were put together at parties, Viola and Jules. They were only a grade apart at school (she was the same age as him, and therefore four times smarter, and didn't she let him know it); their parents were on the same committees, went to the same events, and basically lived inside each other's pockets. There were other kids that belonged to the group, but Viola couldn't stand the Asteria twins, and Jules was far too old to be bothered with Hyperion Locksley and his baby brothers.

When Nicolas Chauvelin joined the Basilisk Board at Belladonna University, he and his glamorous wife Maheen were welcomed into the group with open arms. They brought their children along to the parties, including Sadie, who was in Viola's grade at school but clicked instantly with the hated Asteria twins, Tristan (who was an anklebiter, best locked in the cupboard under the stairs with the Locksley brats), and Ferdinand, who was tailor-made to be Jules' best friend.

Jules despised him instantly.

Parties were more fun after that. Ferdinand Chauvelin made an excellent nemesis. Jules and Viola set the most outlandish magical pranks and traps for him, and he retaliated with creative ingenuity. Best of all, he never told on them to their parents.

Chauv's pranks were devastating. He invented whole new forms of magic just to turn Jules' hair green, and transform Viola's favourite shoes into kittens (which she kept because, kittens).

By the time Viola was twelve (she had skipped another grade by then, because she was more brilliant than even she had imagined), making war on Ferdinand had lost its charms. Coincidentally, that was the year that their parents suggested that the three of them really needed to widen their social circle.

Out of sheer rebellion, they united as a trio of eternal friend-ship, solid and unbreakable.

Chauvelin's magic tasted like electricity, like chaos and power and gold-threaded silk. Viola could still taste his presence in a room, hours after he had left.

This time last year, Viola had known exactly what their future held. She was going to be a dazzlingly brilliant theorist, a professor by 25, tenured and published by 28. Jules was going into hex design, harnessing his destructive powers to their maximum capability. He had already been head-hunted by several companies to work for them after he graduated in November; he wouldn't be bothering with postgrad yet, though he promised Viola faithfully he would come back at 30 to get his doctorate, so as not to fully waste his talents.

Chauvelin was their shadowmancer. Grey Ops had already staked a claim on him, though Professor Hekate and Viola had been working on him to stay a little longer at the university after graduation, because his laboratory work provided such exciting results. He had been published twice already. For most of last year, he had practically designed his own curriculum.

If only they had got to him earlier — if only he had skipped a few grades as Viola had, he might have got so much further in his work, before…

Well. Perhaps the accident would have only happened earlier.

"Hey," said Jules. "The band's starting."

"Curse me now," groaned Viola. But she collected her drink and returned to the table with him.

She loved Ferdinand Chauvelin more than nearly anyone else in the whole world. He was her friend, and she wasn't going to lose him just because he wasn't magical anymore.

Even if he had lost himself.

CHAPTER 4

9PM, I HATE THAT SONG SO MUCH RIGHT NOW

BELLADONNA UNIVERSITY HAS ALWAYS HAD The Band.

It's like this: Belladonna U has always had a student band that somehow achieved 'The' status, thanks to an unholy combination of local in-jokes, hometown support, and indefinable charisma. Some of The Bands go on to national success (Harpy Riot, Owl By Night, Siren), some of them vanish without trace (Second Hand Cauldron, Circe's Sons, Mephistopheles).

When Viola Vale was a firstie, The Band was Kraken, and they were off the hook. Their sound was edgy hard rock, but the lyrics were smart and sassy, full of intellectual wit and old school magical credibility. Viola loved them.

Then they all graduated, a couple of years back, and it wasn't Kraken at Medea's Cauldron on a Friday night any more, it was this lot. Fake Geek Girl, a cluster of nobodies singing about Unreal culture and mixing it up with witch tradition as if that was somehow a normal thing to do.

Viola had no interest in the message they were selling, and that was before they stole her friend.

"Ugh, I hate this song," said Hebe Hallow, which was the first time all night that Viola liked her a little. "I swear Holly only includes it to wind me up."

"It's a classic," Chauvelin teased her.

"It's depressing."

"I think it's supposed to be funny."

Viola frowned, paying attention to the lyrics instead of the conversation. Ten Steps to Survive the Zombie Apocalypse? Ugh. They couldn't pay her to listen to this kind of rubbish.

Everyone knows that if the world is going to end, it will be with ice and trolls. Or possibly dragons.

That gave her an idea for her Hesiod paper, and she slid a pen out of her pocket to jot a few notes on the back of the nearest beer coaster. Unreal technology was mostly an annoyance, but Viola did appreciate the invention of the biro. Imagine if they were all still juggling quills and ink!

When she finally stopped scrawling, she had a neat stack of five annotated coasters, and the only other person left at the table was Hebe Hallow. Viola glanced around for the boys, realising as she did so that Hebe must have been the one handing her fresh coasters.

Usually it was Jules who did that, since the one time she wrote half an essay plan across the back of his designer shirt.

"They're dancing," Hebe said with a soft smile, nodding to where Jules and Chauv were making a disgrace of themselves to a song about dice (had she misheard that?) and 'bitches'.

"Best not to let them know we've noticed," Viola said, capping her pen. "If they think we're watching, they'll grind harder."

"You don't like me very much, do you?" noted Hebe as if it was a passing thought, and not the theme of the evening.

"Don't take it personally. I don't like people." Viola shoved the coasters in her handbag for later. "I have a paper I should be working on," she admitted. "I would be just as rude if I didn't have something better to do, but…" There was no but.

"I'm sure Ferd would understand if you need to head back to the halls."

Viola narrowed her eyes. "Are you trying to get rid of me?"

"Wow." Hebe let out a shocked laugh. "You *really* don't like people."

"You were right the first time." Viola kicked her bag under the table. "It's just you."

She stood up, marched across the pub to where the worst band in the world was playing what had to be one of the top ten worst songs of all time, and hurled herself hip-first at Jules Nightshade.

He caught hold of her, dragged her in between himself and Chauvelin, and they began to dance like they used to, the three of them, before everything went to hell.

"See," growled Chauv in her ear. "Not so bad, is it?"

Viola danced harder, and faster.

———

SHE WAS in bed with an artist when she heard the news. D (she never bothered to learn more than an initial, it saved time) was tall and broad in all the right places, he knew how to keep his mouth shut, and he was excellent with his hands. He had approached her in the library, requesting to sketch her for a series of sculptures he was building of terrifying mythological women.

After witnessing the savaging Viola gave a first-year librarian about the correct regulations on inter-library loans, D thought she would make an excellent gorgon.

It was the best chat up line Viola had heard all year. She allowed him an hour or so with the pencil before she gave him an arch look and started removing items of clothing.

It had been a very good weekend.

She was on the verge of kicking him out of her bed and back to whatever corner of Belladonna U was reserved for finger-painters when the message came in over every mirror in her room.

URGENT
CALL ME

Viola kicked out the slayer of gorgons and connected a mirror call while trying to locate a fresh pair of knickers. "What is it, Nightshade?"

His face flickered before her, taking in her crumpled lingerie and sex hair before he covered his eyes. "Bloody hell, Vale, give me some warning next time."

"Talk faster."

"There's been an accident in the thaumaturgy labs. They've been evacuated."

Huh. "What's the gossip? Chauv should know."

"Vale." Jules sounded deadly serious. "He wasn't evacuated with the others, and he won't pick up my calls."

Heat flickered inside Viola's ribs, where she kept her feelings. "Doesn't mean anything."

"Will you call his mother for me? They might have told her something."

"Call her yourself."

"She hates me."

The flames in her chest were subsiding. "She hates everyone, it's one of the things I respect most about her."

"Vale."

Viola took a deep breath. "Stand by."

And she called Chauv's mother.

CHAPTER 5

10PM, THE BAND TAKES A BREAK

FINALLY, Fake Geek Girl stopped playing their inane songs for an intermission. Viola took the opportunity to escape the stifling pub for a few minutes without looking like a bad sport.

There was an autumn chill in the air and surprisingly few smokers gathered on the back steps. Viola sat down and breathed, letting all the tension from being Polite To Idiots flow out of her fingers and into the cool concrete step.

The pub door opened again, a wash of warmth and noise swirling out before it clanged shut, and a large slab of magical tornado moved past Viola's bubble of personal space.

She called him That Drummer when Jules was around (Jules with a crush was always hilarious) but the truth was, she had a lot of reasons to know who Sage McClaren was.

Sage was a third year student at the College of the Real. A nobody from nowheresville who had more natural magic in his little finger than most of the students put together.

He didn't know anyone. He hadn't taken part in any of the right clubs or camps — his resume was a mess, and he sure as hell would never be invited to join the Basilisk Club. But he was a genius when it came to magical interrogative practice, he had a devious mind for hex design, his last mythology essay had been flawless, and his practical exams often ended with a window exploding.

How could some random country hick in ripped jeans and flannel have so much power when Chauvelin had lost everything? Even if Sage McClaren wasn't the drummer in her least favourite band, even if he wasn't Chauv's new flatmate in that precious little indie commune of theirs, even if he knew how to wear a suit under his academic robes (which he didn't), Viola would have hated this boy with everything she had.

There was no way he wasn't going on to postgrad. They would be colleagues next year, competing for grants and making nice over wine and cheese. She'd have to learn to be polite to him, or die trying.

As long as he and Jules didn't end up screwing, she could cope with his presence. Sucking it up and seething was something she had got good at, over the years.

Sage McClaren lowered himself to the step beside her, shoulders and legs sprawled wide like he deserved all the space. Magic sparked off him, as well as another, less definable energy — from the music, perhaps? He held a full latte glass and cupped his large hands around it, though he didn't take a sip. "Hey," he said. "Vale, right? Ferd wants us to hang out later."

Viola gave him a filthy look.

Sage recoiled. "Whoa, that's familiar. Have you glared at me recently?"

"We're in the same department. I gave a guest lecture to your study group two weeks ago. There may have been glaring."

"Nah, that's not it," Sage said easily. "Something — huh. Why am I thinking about snakes? It will come to me."

"Don't hurt yourself."

The door slammed open again, and a couple of blank-faced bros clutching stubbies leaned over the railing above them.

"Oi, mate, got any Troll to sell?" one of them demanded.

Sage laughed. Apparently being mistaken for a drug dealer was not something that offended him. "That shit'll kill you," he warned.

"Worth it, mate."

"Can't help you."

"Whatever." They wandered away.

"You make no sense," Viola said crossly. His coffee smelled amazing. Why wasn't he drinking it?

"Oh sorry," Sage mocked her. "Did you have some Troll to sell him?"

She narrowed her eyes. "Why are you and your friends being so nice to Chauvelin? What do you expect to get out of this takeover bid of yours? If it's money or influence, he had a lot more of both those things before you got your hooks into him."

Sage sputtered at her, his freckled face hanging open. "Wow," he said finally. "You're a piece of work."

"I'm a realist," she said haughtily. "Sooner or later he'll wake up and realise who his actual friends are."

"Uh huh," said Sage, unimpressed. "If that's true, where have you been for the last few months?"

Flames ran across the backs of Viola's hands. She slapped them away, angry at herself. She didn't usually lose control like this. "We didn't go anywhere," she snapped. "We're not the ones that changed."

"Wow," said Sage again.

"I don't mean him losing — *gah*," she said furiously. She hated being this close to him. So much magic in one place — his and hers, shoving against each other, burning away inside their skin. In another century, they would have been duelling by now. If he was even slightly into girls, she would have her bra off already. "Aren't you going to drink that?"

"Nope," said Sage, inhaling the scent from his latte glass. "Can't consume caffeine right now, or I'll lose my spark for the second set. I bought it for the smell."

"You need magic to hit a few drums with sticks?" Viola mocked. "That seems like overkill." If he wasn't going to drink the damned coffee, maybe she should — at least then only one of them would be brimming over with unchanneled magical energy, and they might not blow this alley to kingdom come.

Sage said "Huh," and tensed up beside her. He wasn't paying attention to her, that was for sure. "Looks like they scored some Troll," he added.

The losers from earlier shambled back into Viola's field of vision. They had that familiar glazed look in their eyes, and frost-blue veins pulsing in their necks. Their movements were slow and heavy, every bit as if their limbs were made of stone.

Troll made you strong, and it made you stupid.

"Why does anyone do that to themselves?" Viola groaned. Their world was full of miracle and wonder — so *of course* her fellow idiot humans had figured out a way to turn majestic magical creatures into a recreational high.

Sage got to his feet, flexing and stretching his hands out, like he could still feel the drumsticks between his fingers. "You're crazy smart. What do you do to silence the fizzing in your brain, when you need to relax?"

"Cheap men and expensive vodka," she snapped at him. "How about you?"

Sage laughed like they were friends. The two troll-heads caught the sound and shifted directions, stumbling across the alley towards the steps. "Hot yoga."

Viola refused to believe that. "Not really."

"Nah, coffee and x-box, mostly. Can't have one without the other. I blew up a ton of gaming systems before I learned that trick." Sage was calm, his eyes on the troll-heads as they meandered closer and closer. "We should get inside."

"Why?" Viola drawled. "Do you think they can out-strategise us?"

"I think," said Sage, sounding worried. "I think maybe those dickheads scored their high by licking a genuine troll."

She hadn't noticed, because her magic was already sizzling and sparking at the proximity of another powerful witch, but it was colder in the alley than it should be. The troll-heads had frost patterns spreading from their skin to their t-shirt collars.

"Oh, hell," said Viola, and got to her feet too.

"Matter of interest," said Sage, flexing his hands again. "Did you ever take the elective on Ethics in Magical Street Combat?"

"I went for Latin Elegaic Poetry As Behaviour Charms," Viola sighed. "But I can throw a hex if I need to."

"Good to know," said Sage, three seconds before the actual, real life ten foot stone troll thundered around the corner, with a howl that made the bricks rattle.

CHAPTER 6

11PM, SECOND SET CONTAINS NEW MATERIAL

VIOLA OFTEN WONDERED what sort of person she might be if her mother had lived. Sweeter, perhaps? Softer, certainly.

Her mother loved butterflies. Viola's strongest childhood memory was the taste of her mother's magic, and the colour of butterflies dancing around them in the garden. When Lifen Vale died, all the colour went out of the world.

She wasn't all about beauty and brightness. Lifen taught her daughter to defend herself in combat both magical and unmagical. She taught her how to cook dishes from China even though neither of them were likely to ever live in a house without a live-in chef and housekeeper. She taught her never to expect love or attention or pride from her father, or to blame herself for that.

One of the worst thoughts Viola ever entertained was that her mother's butterflies and bright-coloured magic might have vanished even if she had survived her illness. If she had lived, Lifen would have had fifteen more years of being married to Victor Vale, and that was enough to turn anyone cold and grey.

When Viola was most brutally honest with herself, she knew that if her mother had lived past the age of thirty, she would have transformed into a creature indistinguishable from Irene Nightshade and Mereen Chauvelin, stone-faced witches who lunched with other stone-faced witches and wore designer clothing and knocked back beauty everlasting charms like they were going out of style. Lifen would have become a woman whose greatest achievement in the world was savaging her best friends with subtle, elegant witticisms.

(Perhaps she was that kind of woman already, when her daughter wasn't around.)

Jules' mother was at least entertaining at the theatre, and inclined to share celebrity gossip whenever she collected it. Viola almost liked Irene, most of the time. But Mereen, Chauv's mother, never quite forgave Viola for the prank that brought her garden statuary to life, and the resulting war between the dragons and the gnomes, which resulted in the destruction of an antique samovar.

Their interactions since then had been frostily polite, when Mereen had not completely ignored her existence.

So last year, when Viola and Jules arrived at the hex-recovery ward, only to be swept up in a hug — a genuine hug — by the mother of their best friend, they knew the worst had happened.

"Is he dead?" Jules blurted out.

"Worse," said Mereen Chauvelin, and burst into tears on Viola's shoulder.

———

VIOLA'S MOTHER Lifen taught her how to use hexes as weapons. She taught her how to use a sword. She taught her how to dazzle her opponent with enchantments and hallucinations, how to get the upper hand.

But it was Ferdinand Chauvelin who taught Viola how to throw a punch, how to shrug and kick her way out of the grip of an attacker, and how anything around you could be a weapon, if you thought quickly enough. His sister had once been kidnapped for ransom by a family enemy, who hired nulls in magic-repelling armour to grab her. After that, Chauv dedicated himself to ensuring that the people he cared about were able to protect themselves whether they had magic at their fingertips or not.

Jules, on the other hand, had taught Viola how to walk away

from a confrontation looking unflappable, like nothing had happened. It was his speciality. Once during his first year, he delivered a prepared talk on the mechanics of raw enchantment while bleeding copiously into a handkerchief, after a recent ex responded to the most sarcastic break up speech of all time by punching him in the nose.

Sage McClaren could leave Jules in the dust. He swaggered back on stage and sat at his drum set like a hero victorious, offering the audience a shit-eating grin despite his bruised knuckles and black eye.

Did he need to enjoy himself quite so much?

Viola sat back at the table, knowing that her hair was a lost cause. If she was sitting, no one would stare at the tear in the hem of her little black dress, or the hex-burn she received from friendly fire, when her final blast at the attacking troll in the alleyway intersected with a near-identical blast from Sage.

She was right all along. Their magic was as incompatible as their personalities. They would never be friends.

Viola sipped at the remains of her drink, now room temperature. As the band started up with one of their noise pollution ditties ("We haven't sung this one in public before. This is a love letter to my sister, and the crazy world she lives in.") — a new song, like that was going to be any better than any of their old material — she realised that Jules, Chauv and Hebe were all staring at her.

> *I love you so much that I care your favourite*
> *   show got cancelled*
> *Again*

"Did you…" said Jules, and then shut his mouth, knowing the inherent risks of mentioning Sage McClaren's name in Viola's company. She was the only one who knew about his crush, and she would throw him under the pegasus if it became a) necessary to curb his ego or b) funnier to say something than to not say something.

> *I care that they whitewashed the casting,*
> *And queerbaited the fans*

Hebe Hallow had no such concerns. "Did you get into a fight with Sage?" she hissed, as if she couldn't quite believe it.

> *And they fridged three female lead characters one*
> *after the other*
> *That really sucks*

Viola tidied her hair slightly with her fingers. "Actually, we fought a troll together, and now we're friends for life," she said infusing it with enough sarcasm that they would never believe the half of the sentence that was true.

> *I'm so sorry*
> *And something about spoilers*

Chauv snickered behind his hand. Hebe gave him a startled look. Jules attempted to not look like he was imagining Sage and Viola in some kind of catfight over his virtue, and failed dismally.

> *I love that you care that your game just isn't the*
> *same without mirrors*

"Okay," said Viola, wincing as the band played on. "I think if we're going to rescue this evening, someone's going to have to order shots."

CHAPTER 7

A LONG TIME AGO, WE USED TO BE FRIENDS

"WELL," said Viola. "You look better than I expected. Glad I didn't bother to source a naughty nurse's uniform."

Chauv sat up in the hospital bed, wearing silk striped pyjamas. His dark curls were wild, and he looked epic hungover tired, like he'd been indulging in Nightshade-encouraged shenanigans and debauchery all week.

Except, there had been no debauchery. He was working in the lab, like he was supposed to, when...

"What were you expecting?" Chauvelin replied, unruffled.

"Oh, you know. Something dramatic. Blood and scars and —" Viola mimed the various dramatic thoughts that first ran through her head when she heard the word 'explosion,' and if that didn't show how worried she had been, well.

Viola Vale didn't mime for just anyone.

"Sorry to disappoint," said Chauv. "Mostly I'm sorry you didn't bother about the nurse's uniform."

"It wouldn't have suited you," she sniffed, and climbed on to his bed to cuddle up against his side. "Does it hurt?"

"Not on the outside." He gave her a squeeze. "How did you get in? The hedgewizards were firm about securing me down."

"I have my ways." She wiggled her fingers at him. "A pinch of illusion, a handful of your mother causing a scene in the corridor outside, a healthy bribe to convince Jules to use his innocent face for good instead of evil — for *once* in his life."

"You're not supposed to use magic in a hospital," Chauv told her sternly. "It messes with the equipment."

"They say that about Mirrorweb too, but I caught four different nurses checking their status updates on my way in." Viola snuggled closer. "Better to ask for forgiveness than permission."

"Like you've ever asked for forgiveness for anything in your life." He patted her hair. "What's it like out there?"

"Quieter now your Dad has stopped marching up and down the corridors bellowing — he's been ushered away to some high up office so he can threaten to sue them all with greater discretion. Your mother is — crying. A lot. On Jules, mostly."

"But she hates Jules even more than she hates you," said Chauv in wonder. "I bet she wishes he was here instead of me."

"Yes, she told him that. To his face. He agreed with her, and now she can't stop hugging him, it's terrifying."

"Ha," said Chauv. He wasn't laughing.

"It's okay," Viola said, burrowing her face into his neck. "It's temporary, that's what they're all saying. You'll be charged up and buzzing again in no time."

"Too soon to tell if it's permanent," Chauv corrected her gently. "That's what they're saying to *me*. They're saying don't get our hopes up."

That wasn't good enough. Viola growled beneath her breath. "When won't it be too soon? No wonder your Dad is furious. When can they give you a straight answer?"

"No idea," said Chauv, his voice shaky. "I don't — what if it doesn't come back, Vale?"

"It will," she promised his neck. "Of course it will." She couldn't imagine a world in which Ferdinand Chauvelin had no magic. "Chin up, Chauv. Everything's going to be back to normal, before you know it."

CHAPTER 8
MIDNIGHT, AFTER PARTY

VIOLA's original agreement with Jules did not involve an after party, let alone an after party at That House where Chauv now lived with his new "magic is optional" BFFs. But the battle-fuelled adrenalin from the fight with the troll, and the shots she downed immediately afterwards, made her forget why this was a terrible idea.

She was not going to let Jules bloody Nightshade win the medal for Most Supportive Friend. If that meant going to a party, then goblindamn it, Viola Vale was going to a party.

It all made some kind of sense at ten minutes past midnight, in a haze of dragon's blood shots with gin-and-rosemary chasers.

Chauvelin and Sage-the-drummer lived on the top floor of a terraced house that they and their friends referred to charmingly (please impose as much sarcasm as humanly possible over any use of the word 'charming') as the Manic Pixie Dream House.

Viola didn't get the joke, but she had learned to arch an eyebrow at the sign of any joke she didn't understand, with this crowd who had somehow dragged Chauvelin into their low rent cult.

With Jules' arm wound around her waist, and Chauv pressed warmly against her other side, Viola stepped into the kitchen of the upstairs flat, to be faced with a large, nearly life-size terracotta statue of Medusa, complete with snakes, covered in a creamy turquoise glaze.

Viola glared at Medusa. Medusa glared back with an identical tilt of the jaw.

"Oh," said Sage, with a shit-eating grin. "*That's* where I've seen you recently."

A tiny Japanese girl in enormous glasses jumped out from somewhere (how many people lived in this house, again?) and peered at Viola. "You're the angry gorgon girl!" she declared.

Sage nodded. "This explains so much."

"I thought I was imagining it," blurted Chauv. "But it really does look like you, Vale."

Viola arched her eyebrow so hard it should have made a dent in their ceiling. "I have no idea what any of you are talking about."

Jules leaned in, and oh no, once he got a teasing topic between his teeth, he would never let go, *she didn't like these people enough to let them make fun of her*. She was going to have to set fire to someone. Or the house. Probably someone.

"Nightshade, heads up," said Sage suddenly, and tossed Jules a beer from the fridge.

The combination of being given a drink, and shock that Sage McClaren spoke to him directly (wow, that crush was still going strong, then) made for a very effective distraction. The flatmates grabbed their own drinks, Jules made a snarky comment to Sage about one of their shared classes, and the moment was lost.

Viola avoided Sage's face after that, because she was worried she might display gratitude, and that would be embarrassing for both of them.

Fifteen minutes later, more of their friends rolled in the door, and it turned out that yes, Sage and Chauv's third flatmate was D, the warm-eyed sculptor Viola had hooked up with the day of the accident. She had regained enough of her cool by then to pretend she'd never met him before.

Hebe brought Viola a glass of wine and didn't attempt to make friendly conversation, which made Viola warm up to her a lot. This was the most relaxed that Viola had been at a party for ages — usually she was in the centre of things, dancing or preening, teaming up with Jules (and Chauv, until recently) to dazzle the crowd with their wit and snark.

It had never occurred to her how exhausting all that was. Here, no one expected her to say a word — in fact, given her behaviour earlier, they would probably prefer she did not.

Hebe's rock star sister glared at Viola from across the room. The artist flatmate kept looking like her like he wished he had his sketchbook handy. Chauv was mostly wrapped up in a conversation with Hebe and her friend Mei (the one with the enormous glasses), but he kept glancing over at Viola too, as if surprised she was still here.

Welcome to the club, Chauv.

On the other side of the room, Sage and Jules traded barbs, getting more and more competitive as they tried to prove which of them was smarter or sharper or more dominant. Jules practically vibrated with energy as their magic sparked against each other.

Ex-hausting.

Sage's bedroom door was open, within Viola's line of sight. He had more books piled on and around his bed than she did. She amused herself for a while, recognising the magical texts by their spines and bindings from a distance. Then she stilled. "Is that a copy of Brahmin's Thermotaugic Compendium? They never let you take that out of the library! There are four forms to even get to look at it for fifteen minutes, and that's if you pledge not to breathe on the pages."

"Professor Medeous lent me her copy," said Sage, only looking slightly ashamed.

"I knew you were her favourite!" Jules complained.

Smug, Sage didn't deny it. He waved Viola towards his room. "If you'd rather hang out with the books, be my guest."

She hesitated, but only for a moment. "I can tell you're being mostly sarcastic, but I am taking you up on that offer."

Sage ushered her on.

Viola frowned at him. "If you're not careful," she said as she got to her feet. "You're going to end up my favourite."

Jules let out a small whine of protest, but then Sage laughed, and apparently watching that miracle of nature was more interesting.

Viola rolled her eyes at them both, and marched into Sage's room, letting the door fall mostly closed behind her.

Wine and conversation were all very well, but books were books were books.

CHAPTER 9

1AM, REGRETTABLE THINGS YOU SHOULDN'T HAVE SAID

VIOLA HAD NEVER BEEN ALLOWED MORE than fifteen minutes in the company of Brahmin's Thermotaugic Compendium, and she wasn't going to waste this opportunity. If being in Sage McClaren's bedroom also lessened the possibility that he was going to hook up with her last remaining best friend tonight, then hey, she was a cauldron half-full kind of witch.

She ignored the Kraken t-shirt she found on the floor, because if Sage turned out to share her taste in music, she might actually have to throw him out a window.

Viola had already read what Brahmin had to say about Prometheus and Hesiod, which was how she knew the library regulations on this book inside out, but this was her chance to absorb the entry on Pandora.

She sat on the carpet, leaning half against a stack of Loeb Classical Editions, and half against the bed, reading until her eyeballs felt sore.

Finally the door shifted open to let someone in, and she glanced up to see Chauvelin in the doorway. Perfect. This was perfect.

"Vale," he teased. "You know it's not good for your brain to let it eat books after midnight, that's how curtains get set on fire in rooms that aren't even yours..."

"This could be the answer," she said, stabbing at the book with her pencil, but turning it aside in the last instant, because students who marked up Professor Medeous's private book collection were likely to disappear without trace.

"For your thesis? Are you still letting Hesiod rule your life?"

"The answer for you," she told him, flapping her hands at the book. "I mean, yes my thesis, I just collected three very important new footnotes, but I think your Dad is going about it all wrong, Chauv. All those medical tests and the hedgewizardry and measuring your core levels, they were about your ability to produce new magic, but none of that addressed where your magic went in the first place!"

"Vale," he said quietly.

"I knew something about Pandora had been scratching at my brain — did you know that fourteen different cultures claim that monsters like trolls and gargoyles and dragons came into existence because of some kind of gods-stealing-magic myth? Pandora's jar, the evils in the world, they were the by-products of Zeus removing magic. There are several historically verified cases where magic being lost or removed by force or accident caused some kind of creature or magically charged item — like the grail, and that whole talking sword business in Belgium. Has there been any investigation into what happened to your magic when you—"

"VALE," he said, and there was nothing quiet or kind in his voice now.

Viola looked up, and saw thunder in Chauv's face.

"Have you been — are you another person trying to *fix me*?" he demanded.

"Well, not full time or anything, but it's been on my mind," she said, startled at his reaction. "You can't — I mean, if there was a solution, you'd want it, wouldn't you?"

"This," he growled. "This is why I couldn't talk to you. This is why I couldn't be around you and Nightshade. You're always going to see me as broken. Missing something. Beneath you."

That stung. "We don't think you're beneath us," Viola protested. "Chauv, you were the best of us —"

"You think I'm less than I used to be."

She almost stopped breathing, because obviously — but that was the wrong answer — and she couldn't lie to him, not about this, she could never lie to him about anything, it was annoying how much he —

Saying nothing turned out almost as bad as saying everything in her head.

"This is why we can't be friends," Chauv snapped, and walked away.

The door swung open, and the living room was full of his friends, not looking at her — most of them — but they had heard, of course they had. Jules looked as wounded as she felt right now; everyone else avoided her gaze.

Damn it, she wasn't going to cry.

Slowly, Viola closed the book that still rested on the bed. She picked up the notes she had been scribbling on — oh, one of Sage's notebooks, hopefully he wouldn't mind — and shoved it in her handbag. With her head held high, she walked through the living room, to the kitchen.

She didn't even see Chauv, but she felt the tingling snap of Sage McClaren's magic as he fell into step beside her.

"Are you escorting me out?" she demanded. "I think I can find the door on my own."

Sage reached for a thick plaid coat and yanked it on. "Nah, I got a Mirrorweb alert about a couple more trolls roaming the local streets. Want to bust some heads?"

"You don't have to be nice to me," she said, rubbing quickly at her eyes.

"I honestly just want to explode some trolls," Sage said, and there wasn't a single hint of sympathy in his face. "You seem like an asset."

She sniffled, and decided that if this was happening, she could be benevolent. "Can I bring Nightshade?"

Sage's smile lit up the room. He was just so sincere. How did Jules not want to put a pillow over his head and smother him to death? "Sure. More the merrier."

By the time Viola learned that 'more the merrier' also

included D the artist, it was too late to say no. She was far too invested in getting to throw some more hexes tonight.

CHAPTER 10

2AM, ILL-ADVISED HOOK UP

TROLLS ABSORBED MAGIC. You couldn't kill them, no matter how many hexes and curses you slammed into their ice-cold, rock-hard skin.

You could slow them down. Every piece of magic they absorbed made them slower, dumber. Like hitting a punching bag that got heavier with every punch. Viola should have been doing this for stress relief weeks ago.

Her magic lit up the night, flaring in the narrow street. She could smell the familiar, icy tang of Jules' magic — which dazed the trolls even more, his magic was chamomile tea to them — and the static, vibrant charge in the air that she could now identify as belonging to Sage.

Trolls weren't allowed in built up areas, which meant someone had brought them here — either to cause trouble or to make drugs, possibly both. According to Sage's sources, this was happening in various suburbs all over the city tonight, not only their sleepy little Hemlock Square and the six block radius that everyone counted as the Belladonna University district.

The police never had enough hex workers on duty, especially night shifts, and Urban Invasion of Magical Beasts was one of three official situations that allowed for vigilante action.

Viola had miscalculated badly. Exploding trolls with hexes in open streets was fun, and served to blow off any Chauvelin-related steam she had built up over the evening. But she had failed to identify the most obvious risk.

She felled the last of the frost-streaked monoliths with a tidy bit of cursework, only to turn around and spot Sage McClaren crowding Jules up against a brick wall so they could make out with each other.

"Give me strength," she muttered.

A flash lit up the alley, as someone clicked her photograph. Viola turned, and glowered at the photographer.

Declan. Dec for short. D the artist had a real name now. Being Chauv and Sage's roommate meant he was probably entitled to more than the initial she usually allowed for her one-night stands.

"Haven't you got enough sketches of me?" she said, hand on hip. "You made the sculpture already."

"Sure, the gorgon," Dec said easily. "But do you realise how many mythological creatures are based in some way on the form of angry women? You rock so many different angry expressions. You're like an encyclopedia of rage and fury." He took another picture.

"It's been a hard night," said Viola pointedly.

That got through to him. Dec lowered the camera, looking sheepish. "Sorry. I should have asked first."

That was worse. Now he was hot *and* considerate.

Viola was tired; hex-bruised. Her anger had worn down into a dull crankiness. Jules and Sage were really going for it against that wall, and part of her wanted to give up tonight as a complete 100% bad idea and go home.

The rest of her was too tense, too rattled to sleep, and couldn't help remembering how good Dec's hands had felt against her skin all those months ago, before the world shifted under her feet. Viola always preferred the Real over the Unreal — magic made everything better. Anonymous hookups were her one exception. There was a delicious emptiness about nulls. She loved the physical feel of a body against hers, without the usual flicker and spark of letting someone else's magic into her bed.

When they left, it was like they had never been there at all.

Declan the artist wasn't anonymous anymore, but he was pleasantly null, the silence of his body a peaceful contrast to the frantic fireworks that rolled off Sage and Jules as they ground against each other.

After tonight's drama of broken friendships and terrible music and ice trolls and so much tension she wanted to scream, was it unreasonable for Viola to crave a brief interlude of feeling something other than pissed off at the universe?

"So we're not pretending we don't know each other any more," Declan said, taking her hand in his, smoothing her soft skin with his rougher palms.

"I don't know you," Viola said. "Sculpting me in clay and snakes and placing me in your kitchen doesn't mean you know me." She liked it that way. She was already too tangled up in these people. Any more would be… impractical. Unfortunate. Ill-advised.

His thumbs grazed the underside of her fingers, making her shiver. The adrenalin from the troll fight was starting to wear off. "You know my name now," said Dec. "That's a plus."

"Is it really?"

Behind them, either Sage or Jules had lost their shirt.

"So, that's a terrible idea, right?" Dec asked. "Sage, and your mate Nightshade?"

"It's the worst," Viola agreed. "It may cause the apocalypse."

"Better keep our distance, then. Do you uh, want to go get a coffee or something?" Dec asked.

"No."

"Right, witch, sorry. Want to go back to the party?"

"Anywhere else," Viola said. "Not your place. Somewhere with no people."

Dec considered, and then smiled. Oh, that smile. She remembered it now, warm like honey. Why should Jules be the only person making terrible decisions tonight?

"I might know somewhere," he said.

———

DECLAN LED her back to the sharehouse, which wasn't promising at all, until he unlocked the garage and drew her inside.

Viola was close to puffing up into another exhausting round of rage because come on, did she look like the kind of girl who was up for a quickie against a car boot or a shelf of tools?

She was pleasantly surprised to find that this wasn't a working garage at all; it was Dec's studio. It smelled of clay and wet paper and there was an artificial tang of painter's varnish, but these were all clean smells, lacking in magic. It was an Unreal space, and she liked it.

Past a series of half-finished sculptures and crates of materials, he led her to a daybed covered in a dropcloth and actual throw cushions. A cosy nest, and more than satisfactory. A man who valued throw cushions was a rare prize. She should seduce art students more often.

Dec was still holding her hand. She could live with that. "I would like to use tonight's photos as references, if you'll let me," he offered.

Viola rolled her eyes at him. "What kind of monster am I going to be this time?"

"I was thinking Amazon, maybe sphinx. Artemis' murderous nymphs if you keep looking at me like that…"

She preened. "Make sure you get my most murderous side. Later, though."

"Later?" he teased.

Viola pushed him down on the narrow bed. The mattress was old beneath the white dropcloth, and it squeaked in protest.

"Later," she confirmed, and climbed into his lap.

When he kissed her, there was silence, blessed silence, in her head and in his.

All terrible ideas should taste this good.

CHAPTER 11
3AM, CLEARING THE AIR

"So," said Dec, much later. "It's because I'm friends with the band, right?"

Viola went very still. "Excuse me."

"Don't worry, I'm used to it. You know. The Fake Geek Girl groupie thing. It's surprisingly effective on bookish girls. Once they figure out Sage isn't straight, and Holl is genuinely not that geeky, and Juniper doesn't do casual, they zero in on their friends."

She was naked and wrapped in a drop sheet that, now she came to look at it closely, was spattered with paint. She was already far outside her comfort zone. But this — presumption was so outrageous that she couldn't even respond, for several seconds.

As she worked herself up to burning fury, Viola realised that Dec was shaking with laughter.

"You," was all she managed to sputter.

"Sorry. Thought it would break the ice."

"Pretty sure we did that fifteen minutes ago," she said, without her usual sharpness. (The sex had been very good)

"True," he said, nudging her shoulder with his chin. "But I have a short window here to make an impression on you before you lose my number and never speak to me again, so."

"You thought terrible jokes would do it?"

"I tried to be all sexy and aloof last time, and you didn't call."

She sat up, wrapping the sheet around her. If that removed some of the cover from him, well. He was the one treating this like an audition. "Don't take it personally. I don't like to repeat myself."

Dec spread his hands wide. "And yet."

"I fought four trolls earlier. I'm treating this as a nights of exceptions." She eyed his bare chest. "And I can't lose your number this time. I don't have it."

He waggled his eyebrows. "Want me to paint it somewhere?"

An electronic chime blared. Dec rolled over, and just like that, they weren't flirting any more. "Damn. Flatmate drama. I've got to go."

"Go where?" Viola asked, searching for her knickers.

"Not far."

THE PARTY, if it could still be called that, had taken to the lawn behind the Manic Pixie Dream House. Some arsehole in a drop dead gorgeous designer suit was yelling at Sage and Chauvelin, who had him cornered away from the house.

Hebe and a couple of other women from the party gathered around her twin sister. It was clear from their own contribution to the yelling that they were equally invested in giving the bloke a hard time.

Jules was there, sullen and dishevelled. His shirt had been buttoned in a hurry, and his hair product had dissolved into the night. Viola, who had reluctantly accepted a plaid (plaid!) flannel (flannel!) shirt from Dec to throw over her little black dress, went to Jules immediately and rebuttoned his shirt.

Even on a night of exceptions, one had to have standards.

Dec went to join the manly group of male protectors, adding his voice to their neighbour's future noise complaints.

"Interesting look for you," Jules said slyly.

"Shut up," said Viola, tweaking his collar. "We're going home. This is not our bullshit."

There was less shouting now, but plenty of angry gesticulating.

Hebe left her sister's side and came over, looking tense. "Holly's ex is making trouble. I really wish she'd start dating girls again, because she has the *worst* taste in men."

Viola nodded like she was interested. "Which one's Holly again?"

Hebe looked dazed. "She's the famous one. Everyone on campus knows who Holly is."

Viola shrugged. "Sure, but was she on the honour roll for Unreal Literature last year? Was her paper about gendered interpretations of Charlotte Bronte published in the *Belladonna Siren*?"

Hebe's mouth fell open. "Did you... stalk me?"

Stalk was such a harsh word. "I researched you," Viola corrected. "I like to know about people, especially those who date my friends. You could have been anyone."

Hebe stared at her for a moment. "Okay, you two, come with me." She raised her voice slightly. "Ferd, I need you!"

Hebe had Chauvelin better trained than any of his previous girlfriends. He left Sage and Dec to deal with the trainwreck ex, and came trotting over. "What's up?"

"Inside," said Hebe. She led the three of them into the ground floor flat, which was some kind of shrine to Fake Geek Girl including band posters, an open box of t-shirts, and flyers for their next gig. "Bedroom."

"This is so sudden," drawled Jules.

With surprising grit, Hebe escorted them into a tidy bedroom that featured no Fake Geek Girl memorabilia whatsoever. She then marched out and slammed the door behind her. The familiar hum of a locking charm sounded in Viola's ears, along with something else... a background magical resonance that had been buzzing at her since she walked into this flat.

"Oh, come on!" Chauvelin groaned. "Hebe, no."

"Hebe yes. You miss your friends! Sort it out, Ferd," she said through the door.

"You realise that I have two of the most talented magical students in Belladonna U's history in here with me," he growled at the door. "I love you, but your locking charms are rubbish."

There was a moment of silence. "You love me?" Hebe said through the door in a very small voice.

Well, this was awkward.

Chauv looked like someone had walloped him over the head with an anvil. "Um," he said.

"No," said Hebe with greater determination. "We'll talk about that later. Viola and Jules might be perfectly able to break my locking charm, but I'm pretty sure they want to have this out with you."

"She's got that right," said Jules.

Viola arched an eyebrow.

"Come on, really?" said Chauv, looking betrayed. He turned back to the door. "Hebe, you and your friends have to learn that you can't solve all your problems by locking people in rooms!"

"Watch me," said Hebe. "I love you too, Ferd. I do. But I am not going to the opera with you. And everyone who lives in this house is scared of your mother. You need your old friends back in your life. Talk to each other instead of yelling and avoiding. I'll be back in half an hour."

Chauv listened to his girlfriend walk away, then turned around. "Let us out."

Viola crossed her arms. "No."

"Are you really going to use my lack of magic against me here?" he demanded.

Jules draped himself on Hebe's bed. "Hey, first rule of friendship, don't piss off the new significant other."

"Sure, you're on her side now," said Chauv.

That buzzing was still in Viola's ear. Something in this room was reacting against her magic. Something cold — but not like Jules's familiar frost and ice. Another, more intrusive magic. She ran her eye over Hebe's wardrobe, and the clothes hanging there.

"Why did you even hang around this late?" Chauv complained, then did a double take. "OMG."

"Did you just say OMG aloud?" Viola snarked. "These people are having a terrible effect on you. You've gone whimsical."

"You both got laid tonight," Chauv accused.

Viola and Jules glanced at each other. Yeah. The signs were pretty obvious. Jules was more relaxed than he had in weeks. And there was no coming back from whatever Sage McClaren had done to his hair in that alley.

"That's not relevant," said Viola. "You're being a dickhead, shutting us out of your life. Why couldn't you just *tell* us to leave the magic thing alone? We're not complete bitches."

"Not all the time," Jules agreed.

"It was hard to come to terms with what happened," Chauvelin admitted. "The hardest thing I've ever done. I needed to not be around you, or anyone else from my old life."

The stabs kept coming. "Is that a forever thing?" Viola asked. "Because that is unacceptable to me."

"I don't know."

"Can we check in with you on a bimonthly basis to see if you're ready to let us back in?"

Chauv's mouth twitched. "Is there a form for that?"

"I am willing to design one."

"Vale's presenting a paper at the conference on Monday," Jules said, unexpectedly. "It's a big fucking deal. Want to come listen and make fun of her afterwards?"

Chauvelin looked desperately uncomfortable. "I can't — that's right in the middle of the College of the Real, Nightshade. I haven't been back there in a long time, I don't — I don't think I can."

"It's fine," Viola said. "It doesn't matter. What about lunch? Weekly. Neutral territory. You, me and Jules. Occasionally with girlfriend. She isn't terrible."

"Wow," said Jules. "Do you know how long it's been since she's deemed one of my partners as not terrible? Take the lunch, Chauv."

Viola whirled around and pointed at him. "You. Your choices *are* terrible. We will be discussing drummer-related hook ups later in this meeting."

"We're going to need a separate meeting for that, because I have *so many* details to share," said Jules with a wicked grin.

"My flatmate, Jules," Chauvelin whined. "Really?"

Jules snickered. Viola pasted an innocent expression on her face.

"Weekly lunch," Chauv agreed. "And... Friday nights?"

Viola's face fell. "No."

"Come on, Vale," Jules encouraged. "Music, drinking, dancing..."

"Dancing to that band? Every single week? No."

"Friday nights once a month, and you don't have to arrive until the second set?"

Boys were horrible. "But I hate their music so much," Viola complained. "Seriously, where is that buzz coming from?"

"Where is what buzz coming from?" Chauv asked.

It wasn't in this room after all. Viola broke Hebe's locking charm like it was made of spaghetti, and went on the rampage. "It's in there."

"That's Holly's room," Chauv called behind her. "So, uh, privacy issues?"

Viola pushed the door open. "Which one's Holly again?"

"The famous one," her boys chorused.

She found it on the bedside table, along with a set of keys, pens and small change. A necklace, flat and silver, giving off that buzz of residual magic. "Ugh," said Viola. "Nasty cheap little trinket. Chauvelin, come here and hold this for a second."

He followed her instructions exactly, his large hand folding around the delicate chain, even as he complained about it. "You can buy null cases in packs of ten, I don't appreciate being treated like a piece of lab equipment..."

"Hush," said Viola, and turned the necklace over with the end of a pen, running a swift diagnosis charm over it. "So, Holly Hallow. The famous one. Her ex-boyfriend's evil."

"Not a shock," Chauv agreed. "The last one was something

big in the music industry, I think, a complete dick, but this one's even worse..."

"Sure, whatever," said Viola. "This necklace is part of a summoning charm that has been luring trolls into the city over the last few days."

"That's," said Chauv, and stopped. "Holly has exceptionally bad taste in men."

"Bring that," Viola snapped. "We need to talk to Sage. I'm ending this."

A STORM WHIPPED itself up in the middle of the postage-stamp sized garden. Holly Hallow was at the centre of it, eyes glowing white, and a halo of fury literally licking out from her skin.

"YOU DID WHAT?" she bellowed at her ex boyfriend.

Her friends stood around her, staring, as if they had never seen her perform magic before.

Viola was impressed. She would make an effort to remember Holly's name from now on.

"Baby," said the ex, who lacked a full set of self-preservation skills. "It's nothing for you to worry about. Just business…"

Holly punched him.

With all the magic she had built up, the punch had the power of several cranky ogres and a side-order of sea monster. It collected him hard and sent him flying into the nearest fence.

"What the hell kind of bullshit did you bring into my house?" she howled at him. "Everyone I care about is in this fucking house!"

The earth trembled beneath their feet as the ex raised his head and glared at her. Viola felt him gather his own magic, tapping into the power of the earth to summon, and to smite. How many more trolls were there in the city? How many could he control?

Sage reached out, and took the necklace from Holly's hand,

snapping it into pieces. A toxic blast of magic spun outwards, and into the night air above them.

The ex laughed. "You think that's my only one, McClaren? I've been screwing my way across this city for months, and I've left a token like that on every bedside table. Tonight was only a taste of the power I can tap into as the One True Trollmaster…"

Viola turned him into stone.

Everyone turned and stared at her.

"What?" she said defensively. "Did you want him to finish his monologue? It was boring."

"You can undo that, right?" complained Holly. "Because I want to punch him again."

"We probably need to know more about what he was planning, in case taking him out of the equation doesn't stop the trolls," Hebe said, with rather more tact.

"Fine, whatever," Viola huffed. She turned the slimeball ex back into his human shape with a wave of her hand and turned around to go inside. It was cold, and she really couldn't remember why she had bothered to stay this long.

"Oi, you'll show me how to do that sometime, yeah?" Sage called after her.

"I'll send you the practicum report, you can peer-review it for me by Monday!" she yelled back.

Around the corner, by the door, she saw Chauv leaning against the wall, talking to Dec in a low voice.

"Don't you feel helpless all the time?"

"It's different for me, mate," Dec said easily. "I never had magic. Never needed it, to do the work I love. My Mum was an Unreal Equity activist — got all riled up about the discrimination against the magic-free in our society. My sisters, too. But it never affected me much."

"How do you protect the people you love without magic?" Chauv asked plaintively.

"Maybe you need to trust them to protect themselves," Viola broke in. "That's what partnership is all about, isn't it? Balancing out each other's strengths and weaknesses?" She almost sounded like she knew what she was talking about. But it worked for academic group projects. Why not relationships?

Both men looked up. Only Chauv looked surprised.

"Easy for you to say," he told her. "You can jump in and help when shit like this goes down. You're not broken."

"My help isn't wanted," said Viola. She glanced at Dec. "You missed me transforming someone into stone. It was amazing."

"I'm gutted," he said. "Next time, give me a head's up."

"I'll devise a special whistle to alert you to my moments of magnificence."

Chauv slouched against the brick. "It's like Hebe only gets half of me," he muttered. "Sooner or later she'll realise that, and she'll leave."

"Ugh," said Viola. "You cannot pull off self-pity, Chauv. Don't even try."

"Dickhead," added Dec. "You wouldn't even have met Hebes if you were still Mr Magic Pants."

"That's true," Viola agreed. "You'd still be with the beautiful people, swanning around with a different girl every night, and never taking them home to meet your parents in case one of them turned out to be Suitable Wife Material."

"Such a life you lead," Dec marvelled. "I've missed so much by not being born into High Society."

Viola could feel magic shifting nearby, under her feet, around the corner. The so-called Trollmaster was at it again, putting up a fight. Part of her wanted to help, though she hadn't been appreciated last time she tried.

"Do you know what I want right now?" she asked.

"Me," said Dec. "Or ice cream."

"A time travel potion so you could go back and tell Jules NO to going out tonight?" Chauv suggested.

"Tonight didn't turn out so badly," Viola admitted grudgingly. "We're friends again, aren't we?"

"Yeah," said Chauv, and took her hand. "Yes."

"Good, then you can make me a cup of coffee. You can't tell me you didn't take your fancy coffee plunger with you when you sneaked out of your family home in the dead of night. Not after you risked being disinherited to smuggle it into your family home in the first place."

Chauv blinked at her. "Coffee. Seriously?"

Coffee would make her vulnerable. Coffee would make her as close to a null as she was ever going to get, barring accidents. Coffee sounded really good right now.

"Ferdinand Chauvelin. Make me a cup of coffee."

———

"POLICE ARE HERE TO ARREST WHATSISNAME," Dec announced some time later, gazing out the kitchen window.

Viola held her empty cup out, and Chauv poured from his stainless steel, stovetop masterpiece. This was her third cup, and it was wonderful. Her magic was muted now, barely accessible, and that made her tastebuds even more alert to the rich smoothness of this particular blend.

"How did they restrain him in the end?" she asked in a bored voice.

"Hebe transformed some broken tree branches into ropes, Sage charmed them, and then after he broke out of that and summoned two more trolls to attack them, Nightshade carved some runes on the grass, and…" Dec leaned out the window to yell, "*You know I really liked that apple tree!*"

"Hmm," said Viola. "If only someone could have turned the villain into stone to keep him available for the police without three escape attempts that destroyed half your back yard."

"To be fair," said Chauv. "That shed was on the verge of falling down anyway."

"This isn't even the most property damage that one of Holly's exes has left us to deal with," Dec agreed.

"That's the trouble with witches," said Viola. "We assume that magic will always be around to fix things. That we are invulnerable. It is a dangerous assumption." She raised her cup in a quiet salute to Chauvelin. "You taught me that. After Sadie was kidnapped by those nulls."

"I remember," Chauv said softly. "I was so angry that they had used our reliance on magic to attack our family. But when Mother found out I arranged for Sadie to have Unreal self defence lessons, she was even angrier. As if me admitting we had a weakness was worse than outsiders using it against us."

"So the occasional cup of coffee won't kill you?" asked Dec.

"Not when we have valiant friends to keep the monsters at bay," Viola said, and saluted Chauv with her cup.

CHAPTER 13
5AM, CRASH SPACE

VIOLA STOLE SAGE'S KRAKEN SHIRT.

It was a perfectly justified action.

The party was over, the police had taken the (ugh) Troll-master into custody, and it was slightly too early to get a decent breakfast anywhere. It was taken as read that everyone would spend what was left of the night here, in the flat shared by Sage, Chauv and Dec. Holly, Hebe and their bespectacled flatmate Mei fetched pyjama party supplies from downstairs: comfortable clothes, spare pillows, and three jumbo bags of marshmallows.

Viola was handed a pair of pyjama pants with owls on them, an over-sized t-shirt with cupcakes on the front (the cupcakes had faces), and was pushed into Sage's room to 'ditch the little black dress.'

This was practically an open invitation to shove the cupcake monstrosity under Sage's pillow, steal his Kraken t-shirt, and button Dec's flannel shirt over the top of it for the sake of subtlety.

Sage was all right, but he was still the drummer in That Band, and he didn't deserve a t-shirt this cool.

WHEN SHE EMERGED WEARING the very latest fashion fusion of flannel and owls, Viola found the whole mess of them — her friends and Chauv's friends — tangled together over couches and beanbags, all limbs and marshmallows, watching the first episode of something trashy on their big screen TV. Chauv was braiding Hebe's hair. Sage and Jules sat as far from each other as they could get.

Viola considered the seating options for a few moments, and then she placed herself directly on Dec's lap.

He grinned, and slung an arm around her waist. "Are you new to *The Bromancers*? Do I need to wiki you the basics?"

She wrinkled her nose at him. "I have no idea what you are talking about. Can we assume I don't care?"

"This isn't the first episode," Hebe exclaimed suddenly. "It's the third episode."

"It's the first good one," Dec called across to her.

"Lies and slander, the first good one is Season 2, the Halloween body swap," said Sage.

"There's lots of great stuff in Season 1," argued Mei. "You can't skip all the meaningful looks and slash potential because you want to cut straight to the episodes with meta-references to existing fanfic."

"Ugh," said Holly. "Why do I even hang out with you people? Can't you just watch a show without all the diagrams and opinions? You'd invent a shipping war out of the Home Cauldron Channel."

There was a pause. "Yeah," said Sage. "But you know those two ladies selling dried potion ingredients are totally hot for each other. I bet there's fanfic."

An argument broke out, which led to half the room unironically throwing popcorn at the other. Viola tried to put up a low level barrier charm, because she was going to get a whole lot less friendly if she ended up with corn in her hair. Her fingers were fuzzy and she stared at them. Oh. Coffee. Damn it. She was going to have to rely on dirty looks to protect her hair from popcorn.

"So," said Dec in a low voice, leaning up to her ear. "Confession time. I collect vintage board games. I'm into role playing, not in the bedroom, well maybe in the bedroom, but I mean a gaming thing. I spend a lot of time working out statistics about fictional dragons. That's often a deal-breaker for women."

Viola rolled her eyes and shoved him lightly. "I translate Ancient Greek poetry for fun, I regularly alienate everyone around me with my pure, unadulterated bitchiness, and I don't do relationships. I genuinely don't care how you spend your spare time."

Dec nodded. "I think you might be my muse."

"That's not a selling point," she informed him.

"I'm willing to invest in an extremely high thread count in bedsheets?"

"That's more enticing."

"So, coffee sometime? Or, a less witch-sensitive beverage of your choice if there are active trolls in the area?"

It wasn't every day you found a boy who looked into the face of a gorgon, and decided he wanted to spend time getting to know her.

"I'll consider it," said Viola Vale.

CHAPTER 14

6AM, BEST HANGOVER BREAKFAST IN THE CITY

"You," said Jules, lost for more intelligible words. "You —"

Viola sipped her tea calmly, and ate a corner of her raisin toast. "We're not going to talk about this," she informed him.

"Vale," he hissed. "You are wearing comedy pyjamas in *public*."

Sometime between 4 and 5 am, Viola had hit a very mellow, philosophical frame of mood, and had somehow managed to stay there despite the people in her general vicinity.

It was all that had kept her going through the screening of an entire episode of *The Bromancers*, with associated commentary.

Jules shut his mouth, surprisingly. The two of them were perched at the counter of the Fennysnake Cafe, which opened at 6am and served what Sage called The Best Hangover Breakfast In the City, what Holly called, Heart Attack on a Plate, and what Hebe called The Least Offensive Option, seriously, The Other Place That Does 6AM Breakfasts is Run By Goblins.

Everyone else was crowded around a mass of tables shoved together, arguing loudly over who was going to order three kinds of bacon, who was going to order what kind of waffle tower, and whether a smoothie counted as breakfast.

None of them had complained or teased when Viola and Jules set up their own little island of calm away from the chaos. That was… surprisingly cool of them.

"He seems happy," Jules muttered into his freshly juiced glass of brightly-coloured pulp. "That's annoying."

"Yep," said Viola, lining up her remaining slices of toast. "Almost like he has this whole life thing figured out."

"He doesn't need us any more."

"No," she agreed. "But he's not shoving us away. So, progress?"

"Progress," Jules agreed sadly.

They sat in blissful lack-of-conversation for a while, as the table of aggressive breakfast debate behind them continued to heave and rattle.

"I always figured you and Chauv would end up together," Jules confessed.

Viola almost choked on her tea. "You thought what?"

"You're both hot and mostly straight, and I don't know. I ship it."

Viola bit savagely into her toast. "You can't just point two straight people at each other and say 'now, kiss,' Nightshade. It doesn't work that way."

Jules lay his head on her shoulder. "But you'd make such pretty babies," he whined.

"Just because you've always wanted to marry Ferdinand Chauvelin does not mean I do!"

He stilled against her. "Low blow, precious."

"I know. Sorry."

"He'd make a terrible husband," Jules muttered.

Viola patted him on the head. "So would you, darling."

Over at the table, Hebe let out a sudden yell. "Sage, it's the song!" she shrieked.

"Shut up," said Sage, shifting in his chair.

"No, wait," said Chauvelin, vaulting over the unholy combination of tables to get to the cafe's little radio. He turned it up.

"Wait," said Viola, tilting her head. "Is this Kraken?"

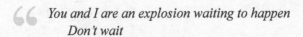

You and I are an explosion waiting to happen
Don't wait

> *Light it up*
> *Let's go*
>
> *I set fire to your broom,*
>   *You'll incinerate my car,*
>   *Flame on,*
>   *This is us*
>   *Burn hard!*

IT WAS A ROUGH, fun song, with that characteristic Kraken sense of humour. Viola hadn't listened to them in ages — hadn't realised there was a new single out.

Sage looked like he had been hit over the head. Obviously a true fan. Too late, Viola wasn't giving the t-shirt back now. Hebe and Chauv giggled and shoved each other while they listened to the song all the way through. When it was over, the whole table burst out into applause.

"See, that's a good song," Viola said, when the noise had died down. "Why don't your band do songs like that?"

Chauv laughed so hard he nearly head-butted his girlfriend in the face.

"I wrote this one," said Sage.

Viola stared at him. "You wrote a song for Kraken?"

"You got paid to write a song that got on the radio!" howled Chauv, and he and Dec fell over themselves to slap Sage on the back. Hebe and Holly threw themselves on his lap, hugging and/or punching him.

Viola observed them thoughtfully.

Finally, Sage scrambled out from under his friends, red-faced and glowing. "How many cool points is that worth, Vale?"

"Fewer by the minute," she said crisply.

Jules laid his head on Viola's shoulder again, looking jealous and pouty. "Which one is Kraken?" he whispered at her.

She squeezed his knee. "Don't worry, Nightshade. You have your looks to fall back on."

PART THREE

MONDAY MORNING AGAIN (STILL)

CHAPTER 15

ADULTING IS OVER-RATED

VIOLA'S PAPER was calm and intelligible and coherent. None of the professors laughed or scowled at her (except for Professor Schumaker who always had 'grumpy' as his default expression even when presented with birthday cake). It was a resounding success.

She was barely aware of that, because *he* was here, watching her from behind those forbidding eyebrows while she outlined the mythical treatment of a world without magic, according to Hesiod and his later imitators.

Every line out of her mouth sounded like a passive-aggressive dig at Chauv, and how he had dealt with his own "world without magic" over the past several months. Every line sounded pointed, or cruel.

Chauv wasn't here to hear it. But *he* was.

Dr. Nicolas Chauvelin, High Quill of the Basilisk Board. Approver of scholarships. Terroriser of admin staff. Legendary shadowmancer. Chauv's father. He never came to student presentations; never came to faculty events at all, at least for as long as she had been a part of the College of the Real. Viola had never exchanged more than two sentences with Dr Chauvelin on campus — most of their interactions were at private family events and consisted of something in the line of "Hello, young lady and how are you going with your studies?"

Somehow she got through her presentation and sat down, hands shaking. Somehow she sat through three other grad student papers, none of which was as thoroughly researched as her own.

Somehow, she survived to morning tea, and stood as an island with a cup of Earl Grey, swarmed by well-wishers. Many of them had a question about her paper, but had not bothered to ask it during the formal time for questions and answers.

(She had been so terrified that Dr Chauvelin would ask a question; so relieved and somehow disappointed when he had not)

"Miss Vale," he said now, approaching in her blind spot. The question-askers took one look at his glowering face, and melted away with polite excuses.

She turned. Jules was nowhere in sight, the coward. "Dr Chauvelin. Are you enjoying the conference?"

He did not bother to make pleasantries. "I think it's time you and I talked about my son, and how to stop him throwing his future away."

Then he talked, and he talked.

———

IT WAS Sage who rescued her, in the end. Sage McClaren, of all people. He swept past, said "Sorry sir, can I borrow Viola for a minute? Vale, Professor Dunkirk needs you, something about an undergrad meltdown in the foyer, one of your students? Have you back in a minute." He swept her up and away through the crowd, firmly steering her with that large, comforting presence of his, until she was outside, in the back stairwell.

Viola choked on the cool, concrete-tasting air, shocked to be free of that awful conversation. "He was saying…"

"I know what he was saying," Sage said grimly. "It's bull-shit, all of it."

"I knew they wanted to bring him in for more tests, but… He's treating this like it's some sort of *disease*, like they can cure

Chauv if he submits to more radical experiments. Which don't sound remotely legitimate, by the way."

"They're desperate. It's nothing Ferd hasn't heard from them already. That's why he cut off contact with his family. They were talking about blood replacement therapy, and some other freaky stuff that's completely against current medical or magical advice. His mother sent him tickets to a Swiss hospice for his birthday. I know they were trying to get some bullshit legal injunction to force his hand…"

"I didn't know it was this bad. His Dad was talking about him like he's barely human now." Viola covered her face. It was hard to breathe. "I tried telling him how well Chauv was doing — that he's sorting his life out."

"Yeah, they don't care about that. They want him to fit back into his old life."

"Like I did," Viola said bleakly.

"Vale!" Jules banged through the stairwell door and joined them on the landing. "Sorry, I thought McClaren had a better chance of getting you away. Maman's been trying to get me to agree to a meeting with Dr Chauvelin for weeks."

Viola's lungs felt tight. "Jules."

His eyes narrowed as he took in her condition. "Oh fuck, let me have it, then." He leaned in.

She slapped him hard across the face, knocking him to the ground.

"Holy shit, what's wrong with you people?" Sage yelped in alarm.

Viola breathed. It was easier now. "It's the best way to stave off a panic attack. I used to get them a lot at school."

"Tried and tested," said Jules, rubbing his face.

"Why is *he* the one getting slapped?" asked Sage.

"Would you slap her? Seriously? Even if she asked?"

Viola bared her teeth at them both. "He volunteered. Indefinitely."

———

THE REST of the conference was manageable. Viola returned to the lecture hall late, flanked by Sage and Jules. Dr Chauvelin did not attend the remainder of the day's presentations, but Viola felt herself constantly looking over her shoulder.

Afterwards, Sage dragged them back to the Manic Pixie Dream House, with a vague promise of Dec cooking dinner. Viola wasn't sure how she felt about Dec or his unbelievable spaghetti recipe, but she knew that she needed to see Chauv.

She needed to hug him around the neck, and say sorry.

Because the truth was —

The truth was that if Dr Chauvelin had come to her a week earlier, she might have agreed that Chauv was throwing his life away, that it was concerning how he had cut all ties from his old life. She might have agreed to help him get his son into treatment, and back into the College of the Real where he belonged.

She had been doing his parents' dirty work for them all along, without even being asked.

"Hey, how was the conference?" Chauv called out when they got to the upstairs flat. Dec was chopping onions, and Hebe was reading something on her hand mirror.

Viola threw herself at Chauv, hugging him hard. "Shut up, you're fine," she snuffled into his chest.

He patted her on the back. "I know I am, Vale. Are you fine too?"

"Work in progress."

"Hey, would the band be up for playing Winterfest out at Mandrake Sands this year?" Hebe asked out of nowhere.

"That depends," sniffed Viola. "Are they planning on getting good between now and then?"

"Ouch!" laughed Sage.

"I apologise for Vale, she skipped two years of manners to get ahead on her spellcasting classes," said Jules.

"That's OK," said Chauv. "We're not looking to change her."

Viola raised an eyebrow at him. "I'd like to see you try."

———

MIRRORWEB EXCHANGE

Subject Heading: Thesis Topic Revisions y/n?

VIOLA VALE: WOULD IT BE WORTH INCORPORATING AN EXTRA CHAPTER IN MY THESIS ABOUT POSITIVE PORTRAYALS OF THE LOSS OF MAGIC IN MYTHOLOGICAL CHARACTERS? SUGGESTING THAT IT ISN'T ALWAYS A SOURCE OF EPIC TRAGEDY?

Professor Ariadne Medeous: Interesting take on the subject. I might have some sources. This will increase your workload. Are you sure you want to risk blowing out your timeline?

I CAN MAYBE WRITE LESS ON THE ROMANTICISATION OF MAGIC IN EARLY LITERATURE? THAT'S A TOPIC THAT'S BEEN DONE TO DEATH.

That sounds like a good plan. Your closing date to lock in your final thesis outline is Thursday, but I can extend that to Saturday if you need more time.

THURSDAY'S FINE. I HAVE PLANS THIS WEEKEND.

Of course, Friday Night at the Cauldron. They've been doing that since I was in undergrad. What's the current The Band like?

ANNOYING. INFURIATING. NOISY. PUSHY. OVERLY INVESTED IN MY LOVE LIFE. ASKING FAR TOO MANY QUESTIONS ABOUT A CERTAIN T-SHIRT. BUT... THEY'RE GROWING ON ME. DON'T TELL THEM I SAID THAT.

THE BROMANCERS

SOUND-MUFFLING HEX BAGS are the most useful item that any university student can invest in. I always have three at a minimum in my bag, at all times.

But the exam hall of the College of the Unreal is long and old and had magic-repelling spells baked into its bricks in the late 1800's. This means witches like me can't use magic to cheat on our perfectly mundane literature or mathematics or engineering or law exams.

It also means we have no way to protect ourselves from the thoughtless antics and distractions caused by our fellow students outside the exam hall.

I was sitting near the window, my lucky essay-writing pencil worn down to the nub. I could hear the raucous popping sound of celebratory fireworks on the other side of campus. The College of the Real was warned on multiple occasions that they weren't allowed to indulge in any noisy magical celebrations until 4:15pm today, when the final College of the Unreal exam concluded. They hadn't listened.

A horde of purple butterflies whooshed past the window, trailing golden streaks. This was followed by a cloud of bats. Someone, clearly, was proud of their work on a Metamorphosis prac.

One student, breaking three different Belladonna University

rules by holding an open beer can while riding a broomstick *shoeless*, swooped past the windows on the far side of the hall. He dropped like a stone when he came too close to the aura of the magic-repelling bricks.

Ouch.

Around me, students were frowning, muttering, turning away from the windows. Every Unreal student in the hall was united in a mass seethe against Them. Our other half.

The sense of entitlement and importance that magical students claim over the unmagical has been a part of this university since its beginnings.

The College of the Real is named that because the university's Founders felt magic was the only important, practical topic that any witch or other magically-inclined person could possibly choose to study.

The College of the Unreal covers the subjects that have nothing to do with magic. Belladonna University claims that all students are treated equally, but the faculty of the College of the Real are just as likely to sneer in our direction as their under-grads. *College of the Unimportant*, they call us. *College of the Unprepared. College of the Why Even Bother?*

I'm a Hallow, which means I'm descended from an old, highly traditional family of witches. Some of my best friends study at the College of the Real. And here am I, majoring in Unreal Literature because as it turns out? Some of the most interesting plays and poetry in the history of the world were not written by witches. The College of the Real doesn't even have a Department of Gender Studies. I was happy with my choice, even if my family were bemused.

Today, I'd written everything it was possible to write on the poetry of Sylvia Plath, and there was still forty minutes left of the exam. I could stand up and leave — the professors never actually get told who stays for the entire time and who takes an early minute.

I know that. But I can still never bring myself to do it.

So I flipped a couple of pages of the exam booklet and

started a draft of the Plan, the same Plan that's been rolling around my head for more than a month now.

- OUR QUEST: to get the indie rock band Fake Geek Girl to the Winterfest campgrounds at Mandrake Sands with all necessary gear to survive a three day music festival. Without anyone murdering anyone else.
- OUR PARTY: Three band members, one reluctant manager substitute (me), 2 volunteer roadies, and X number of significant others. I can't tell you how much I was hoping that X = 0.
- OUR TRANSPORT: 1 van, 1 very elderly VW beetle, several broomsticks.
- OUR GEAR: A drum kit, a cello, three large tents, one small tent, six sleeping bags, a crate of protein bars, a crate of instant soup, 4 broomsticks, 1 enchanted porridge pot (family heirloom), 2 spare cauldrons, a dozen sound-muffling hex bags and a sack of insect repellent charms.

Oh yeah. Someone was definitely going to die.

The trick was figuring out the best possible configuration of people to travel in the same vehicle for several hours, and still be friends by the time we were ready to set up camp. A similar configuration had to be found for the sharing of tents — thank goodness the SOs had agreed to give Winterfest a miss this year, or it would never work out at all.

I had to trust that it would stay that way, that we weren't going to get any sudden 'romantic' surprises. This weekend was about the band, not the drama.

Who was I kidding? Fake Geek Girl was always about the drama.

Our drummer Sage had embarked upon an epic on again/off again enemies-with-benefits relationship/shagging arrangement with Jules Nightshade, who was best friends with my boyfriend

Ferd Chauvelin. Jules and Ferd's other best friend Viola had settled into something romantically undefined with Dec, who was our volunteer roadie as well as being Sage and Ferd's flatmate.

Our lead singer, my twin sister Holly, had managed somehow not to acquire a terrible, world-destroying boyfriend in the last two months, which sounded good on paper but meant she'd be on the prowl this weekend, and could be bringing *anyone* back to the campsite. So that was going to automatically screw up any of the planned sleeping arrangements.

Yeah. I should have hired more tents.

Juniper, the band's cellist, and Mei (my and Holly's flatmate and our second volunteer roadie), did not currently have girlfriends despite my wistful attempts to set them up together.

In an ideal world, I'd put the two of them in the same tent and hope for the best, but that would leave me sharing with Holly and the plan was to avoid murders this weekend. So Holly could have calm, lovely Juniper, I'd share with Mei, Sage and Dec could have a bro tent to themselves, and everything would be fine as long as — and I can't stress this enough — everyone's significant others stayed well away.

———

"IT'S NOT that I don't want you to come," I promised Ferd.

"Sweetheart, I know." He sat on the edge of my bed while I crawled on the floor, redrawing my battle plan for the camping situation on to a poster board. My last version of the Plan was submitted with the rest of my exam, disappearing from my sight forever. (Had I drawn a line through it to indicate it shouldn't be marked? I hoped so!) "Believe me, Hebe, three days in a tent with my flatmates, whatever insects can survive an Australian winter, and a bunch of musos is not my idea of a good time."

I smiled up at him. "It's going to be hell. And you've got — your own stuff to worry about right now."

Ferdinand Chauvelin is the most beautiful man I've ever seen. I wonder sometimes what he's even doing with me — and I know that other students wonder that too, when they see him walking across campus holding hands with my mousy, ordinary self.

Ferd is of French-Arabic descent, his family belonging to the wealthiest elite tier of magicians, and I'm pretty sure that every ancestor in his family tree chose their spouse for glamorous good looks and elegance as well as magical ability. His elite status is signified by the rare, extraordinary magical tattoo across his collarbone and shoulder — a fluttering, animated phoenix.

He's what kids at uni call a Basilisk King — legacy child of the Basilisk Board, born with a silver wand in his mouth. He still wears his signature soft silk designer shirts and thousand-dollar boots, because his family weren't such complete arseholes that they kicked him out without access to any of his belongings.

They did, however, kick him out. There have been a few mirror calls lately, awkward attempts to reconnect, but nothing solid. Nothing he can count on.

"So what are your plans for next weekend, while I'm slumming it in muddy tents with a sleep-deprived rock band?" I asked, moving from the floor to cuddle up next to him on the bed. "Something trashy and indulgent with Jules and Viola? Hot rock spa? Champagne brunch?"

"Why would you assume that a hot rock spa and champagne brunch were separate activities?" Ferd teased. "Nah, I'm, uh." He looked uncomfortable. "I'm actually visiting my parents."

I blinked. "Really? You're going home?"

"Well, lunch at my Aunt Samara's house, which is, yeah. The closest we could get to neutral territory without meeting in some kind of public park or restaurant. But they'll be there. So." He looked anywhere but at me.

"Ferd, why didn't you tell me?" This couldn't be a new development. He'd been on edge lately, and had always excused himself when his mirror pinged with one of those awkward calls. But it had been hard for me to concentrate anything that wasn't about exams, the last few weeks. Was I a horrible girlfriend, that I hadn't pushed him to talk about this? "Do you — I mean, do you want me to come with you?"

"Hell no," Ferd said quickly, and then looked horrified. "I mean. I didn't mean."

"Oh, I get it," I said, trying to sound neutral and not hurt.

It wasn't hard to guess what his family thought about me and our relationship, if they knew about us at all. I'd got a preview of how I rated on the Basilisk scale of importance when I first met Viola, Ferd's snootiest friend, before she came around to accepting me as a worthwhile human being.

I might be a Hallow, which means something in magical circles, but that's a long way from being a worthy girlfriend to grace the arm of a Chauvelin son and heir. It wouldn't help that I was associated with the share house where Ferd now lived, the friends he had made. The friends who helped him come to terms with his lack of magic, after the accident. The friends who supported and encouraged him through his transfer to the College of the Unreal.

Yeah, his parents were going to hate me.

"I meant literally nothing by that," he promised, burying his face in my neck. "Hebe, I'm embarrassed of them, not you. I don't want you anywhere near those people. They would tear you up to score points off me."

"I didn't want you to be alone, that's all," I said defensively. "I'm not angling for an invite."

"Oh, I won't be alone," he said casually, pulling back from me. "Vale's coming as backup."

Of course she was. Viola Vale wasn't just Ferd's friend. She was a woman of his world — the world of money and old magic and fancy board meetings and designer clothes. She knew the right fork to use. She called Ferd's mother by her first name. Neither of them ever said it aloud, but I was pretty sure their parents had always expected them to marry each other.

Viola Vale was everything I was not.

I wasn't jealous. I trusted Ferd. But ever since he stumbled into my life, part of me has been waiting for him to spark the "undo" charm and return to them — to his family, to his whole world, to the person he was before the accident.

When he does, that world of his won't have room for me.

CHAPTER 2

SAGE SAYS: 10 OUT OF 10, WOULD BREAK UP WITH AGAIN

FRIDAY

I HAD this bloody song wriggling under my skin, trying to get out. I had a few lyrics, a theme, and I was maybe halfway to a chorus.

Mostly right now it was rhythm, and that meant thumping out a beat on anything that came near me — walls, beer cans, my thigh, my phone, the long drink of hotness currently stretched out and naked in my bed.

"If you compose a tune on me, I'll claim royalties," grunted Jules Nightshade, his face buried in my sheets. "Too early in the morning for this shit."

"That's what you get for banging a drummer," I said, and laughed at myself, because no one but me was gonna to appreciate drummer puns.

It was like, 11am. But we were students and it was the beginning of our mid year holidays, so. Too early for this shit. Fair call.

"I need coffee," Nightshade muttered.

He wasn't wrong. I found a line of my song somewhere near his spine, and as I tapped out the repeat with my fingertips, his skin sparked against mine. Damn it. We'd downed triple espresso shots at 4am before tearing each other's clothes off, and they were already fading from our systems.

Coffee: nature's own anti-magic ward. The easiest way for two high-grade magic users to tamp down their powers long enough to get messy in the bedroom, without burning the house down.

My sheets dropped in temperature as Nightshade's core of magic — ice powers, of course — began to return. If I kissed him right now, I'd be huffing steam into his mouth like a kid running outside on a winter's morning.

Good thing I wasn't gonna kiss him.

"So," said Nightshade, rolling away from my tapping fingers, and offering me his frostiest glare. His blond hair looked good dishevelled, straight off a pillow. He looked like less of a pretentious dickhead than when he was in his club clothes, all gel-spikes and thousand dollar leather trousers.

Sometimes my taste in blokes embarrasses even me.

I waggled my eyebrows at him. How annoying did I have to be, to get him to voluntarily leave my bed? Maybe I was relying on the wrong technique. If I was sweet to him, would he run for the hills?

We were never gonna know. Neither of us could do 'sweet.'

"So," I repeated, wanting him to get on with it. I had a song to work on.

"So you're going on tour for a week. With your band." Nightshade said the words 'your band' in the same tone someone might say 'your STD.' Like he didn't dance to our sound every Friday night, like he didn't love strutting up to me when I was sweaty and exhausted after a show. Like that wasn't a gleam of possessive want all over his face every time he dragged me away from the other pretty boys that had been giving me hopeful eyes all night.

"Threeeee dayyys," I said, letting the words drag out on my tongue. "Are you sure you don't want to come to Winterfest? Hipster beards and piercings as far as the eye can see. DIY trench toilets and air beds. All-vegan catering. Totally your scene."

Jules Nightshade wouldn't even stay in a three star hotel. I knew my audience.

He rolled out of bed now and started dressing himself in a very familiar haughty air. Oh, we'd done this dance before. "Good time for a break, don't you think?" he said sharply. "Put a little distance between — you know. This colossal error of judgement."

"Aww, baby," I said, folding my arms behind my head and flexing my biceps at him. "Are you breaking up with me?"

Fourth time since April, but I wasn't gonna point that out. Let the man have some dignity.

He hesitated over whether to pull on his own green-cocktail-stained shirt from the night before, or steal one of mine. Night-shade has been systematically stealing band shirts from me ever since the night his mate Vale made off with my prize glory, the 2014 Kraken shirt with an embarrassing misprint.

It's cute, the way he thinks I haven't been keeping track.

But this was a Nightshade Breakup Scene, so he buttoned his own shirt, despite the stickiness. "We don't fit, McClaren. It's too much effort. I'm starting to get caffeine headaches even when I don't see you, so…"

I kicked my doona off, to give him a glimpse of what he'd be missing. Jules huffed at me, annoyed, but that didn't stop his eyes raking down my body, all the way to my morning wood, standing well and truly to attention. "Blow me before you say goodbye," I suggested in a low, husky voice.

"If you put that line in a song, I'm going to fucking end you," he threatened.

I laughed at him, and he left.

On a scale of 1 to 10, it was one of our better break ups.

Hell yes, I was gonna put that line in a song.

————

"ROAD TRIP, ROAD TRIP!" chanted Dec.

I tapped out the bridge of my almost-song against the side of the van while Juniper hauled her cello aboard, nestling it against the camping gear and as far from my drum kit as possible. "Nah, mate. It's not a road trip if it takes less than four hours to get there. This is barely even a weekend drive."

"I don't see why I can't be in the van," Holly complained. "I never get to ride in the van."

Her better half, the twin I would have married already if I was straight, rolled her eyes like a champ and waved her clipboard. Of course Hebes had an honest-to-pixies clipboard. No bet that she bought it new for the trip. "Sage needs to be close to his drums or he gets bratty, and I'm trying to limit the number of possible murders this weekend. Which means you and Sage don't get trapped in an enclosed space together, under any circumstances."

"I blame you for denying me the authentic tour bus experience," Holly said, pointing her finger at me with all the emphasis of a wand.

"Not a bus, one show only, not a tour," I corrected. "We're not even stopping for lunch on the way. This is a camping holiday with a brief gig in the middle. Don't go telling Instagram we're on a fucken tour. It's embarrassing."

"Oh, we're stopping for lunch," said Hebe, her left eyeball twitching ever so elegantly. "If I don't get to eat dirty burgers and potato cakes from a roadside cafe, there is no point to any of this."

"I'm not travelling in that tiny little pixie car," Holly announced loudly, pointing at Mei's VW. "I refuse. Zip me up in Juniper's cello case, I'm travelling authentic."

Hebe gave her sister an unimpressed look. "Broomstick or backseat. Those are your choices."

Hebe was playing hardball. Everyone knew that Holly was goddamned dangerous on a broom. Her magic reacted badly to altitude, and she had all the physical reflexes of a cockatoo on a sugar high.

"But shotgun," Holly whined.

"Broomstick, or backseat."

Fuming so hard her hair was in danger of vibrating away its pink highlights, Holly stalked to the van and snatched her broomstick from our collection. "I hate you all. I'll be there to pick a campsite before any of you roll up."

"I reserved our site!" said Hebe, starting to look worried. Not about the campsite, obviously. She'd had that locked down for months. But the sight of Holly holding a broomstick flashed warning signs in front of all our eyes. Our Hol was the only witch I knew who was less likely to get into a mid-air collision when she was drunk and stoned than when she was sober.

"I'll swap whatever dinky site you picked with the first metalhead I see!" Holly said wildly.

This power struggle wasn't about Hebe, though she was getting the worst of it as always. It was about me. Somehow, with band shit, it always came down to Holly and me, fighting for control.

"Hey," said Dec, playing the peacemaker. "You know the last episode of *The Bromancers* drops this weekend?"

"We know," said Hebe impatiently, like he had mansplained to her that brooms were made of twigs. "It's in the plan. There are some tech problems to work around, but Mei's on it."

"I'm on it!" hollered Mei from the mini. "We'll miss Dark Kelpie opening for Holy Water Hexology, but it's worth it. The bros are so gonna bone in this episode, it's gonna be great."

Holly, waved her broom dramatically, so no one would miss her grand exit. I had a sudden vision of her splattered all over the highway because she was passive-aggressively flying too close to the rest of us.

"Fine," I said abruptly. "Fuck it. You take the van."

Everyone stared at me.

"Sage, I don't think I can fit your drum kit in the Bug," Mei said slowly.

"Drums in the van. Me in the Bug." I faced down Holly who looked bizarrely shocked at getting her own way. "I'm gonna squeeze all 6 foot 2 of my big bad self into the back seat of that tiny little pixie car (no offense, Mei)."

"Fuck you, Sage."

"And you know why I'm gonna do it, Hol? Because I'm a team player."

Holly stared at me, and then she smiled beautifully. Her fake, perfect 'being nice to fans' smile, made brighter by her perfect lip gloss. "Sounds good."

Hebe sidled up to Dec. "Um. Drive carefully," she said in a low voice. "There will be no living with Sage if anything happens to his drums."

"Yeah," said Dec, rolling his eyes at her. "I love you too, Hebes. Your priorities are excellent, as always."

I DON'T BLUFF. By the time Mei and Hebe had finished packing everyone else into the van, I was stretched out in the back seat of the VW. Stretched out may be overselling the concept, but I was going for draped, okay?

Hebe snapped a pic. "That's going on the Instagram."

"I have all your snacks back here and I'm not afraid to eat them loudly right behind your ear," I sniped back.

Mei slid into the driver's seat. Hebe snapped on her seatbelt. "No Jules for this trip?" she asked. "I expected him to invite himself along at the last minute."

"Uh, that's not a thing any more. No big deal." Damn it. Why did I say No Big Deal? That just made it seem like a big deal. I was failing so hard at casual right now.

"Brace yourself, Mei," Hebe said calmly, as we pulled out ahead of the van, making for the highway. "I think our drummer wants to talk about boys."

Yeah, no. Never gonna happen.

———

HERE'S the thing about me and Hebes: we were high school sweethearts. She was the perfect girlfriend, and I would have stuck with her forever if I hadn't had my Big Gay Crisis and thrown myself on her mercy.

We're still friends. Best friends. Which is so much more than I thought I deserved, when I first told her the truth.

But there's some stuff you don't dig into with your ex, even the coolest ex ever. Jules Nightshade was top of that list — lately he was the entire list. That was getting to be a problem. Trust me to get attached to a bloke whose second best talent was breaking up with me.

Though his first best talent almost made up for that.

"So," I said three minutes into our 'road trip'. "You know I'm right about the album, Hebes."

Hebe groaned and smacked herself in the forehead. "You did not wangle your way into this backseat to work on me about that bloody album title. It's between you and Holly and Juniper, you know that."

"My title's the best," I argued. "My song is the best. Holly's only being stubborn because…"

"Because Resting Witch Face is a song about her, Sage. She knows it. We all know it. If it was a flattering song, maybe you'd have more leverage. But you wrote it when you were pissed off at her, and it shows."

"Best song ever," Mei said in an undertone. I caught her eye in the rear view mirror and mimed a high five.

"I don't get a vote," Hebe said impatiently. "I'm not —"

"Hebes, you've been acting as our manager for months now. We did OK without one back when Nora was in the band because she was all Organisa Von Spreadsheet. Once she left, we were a mess until you started, you know. Tidying us up."

"But," said Hebe, sounding genuinely confused. Hopefully it would turn out to be flattered-confused and not chuck-Sage-outta-the-car confused, but I wasn't sure if even she knew yet how she was feeling about this.

"I'm pretty sure, as our manager, you get a say on which song title we use for the album," I said smugly, folding my hands behind my head.

Hebe turned around, and gave me a very pointed stare. "So you and Jules Nightshade. Is this a permanent break up or yet another half-hearted, passive-aggressive bluffing attempt because one of you got cold feet about feelings?"

I accepted her change of subject, but only as a temporary

truce. "Pretty sure it's an excuse for him to get blasted and hook up with other boys while we're away."

Hebe blinked. "We're only going for three days. He can't keep it in his pants that long?"

Remember how Jules Nightshade was on the list of things not to discuss with my ex? This is why.

I gave her a cheesy grin. The sleeping around thing really didn't bother me, but I knew it would bother her. "Maybe he didn't trust me to keep my own jeans zipped this weekend. Either way, I'm free and I don't have to feel guilty about it because he did the breaking up. Can we leave it?"

"Fine," Hebe grumbled, and then added a bunch more grumbling on top of that, which I didn't strain myself to hear properly.

"So," said Mei in the awkward silence that followed. "I'm going to share five of my favourite theories about how this season of *The Bromancers* will end, and you're going to tell me how correct and brilliant I am. Deal?"

———

OKAY, so it wasn't a proper road trip, and I spent nearly four hours crammed into a tiny back seat, but it wasn't all bad. At least we stopped for dirty burgers and potato cakes along the way, so Hebe's mood improved.

This weekend, at Mandrake Sands? It was gonna be epic. I could feel it in my bones, almost as deep as that song I hadn't found yet. All I had to do was convince Holly that Resting Witch Face was the name of our next album, and everything would be gravy.

CHAPTER 3
TRUE BROMANCE, MEI-STYLE

FRIDAY

*You Are Gazing Into the Mirror of **MeMei***
*Who Is... **currently scarfing egg and chips at a greasy spoon on the side of the highway**.*
Add Your Reflections Below!

So I'm roadtripping down to Mandrake Sands this weekend, for social reasons (ugh) and to support my favourite local indie band (hey, download Fake Geek Girl's latest album here, it's on the pay what you want system!).

You know what that means.

I'm going to be away from home when the final episode of Season 3 of *The Bromancers* drops.

EEEEEEEEEEE!

Don't fear, I have Plans to circumvent the ridic 'wi-fi free zone' enforced by the Winterfest Volunteer Committee, and I will be watching that ep come hell, high water, or mutually assured musician destruction.

In other news, how much does it suck that some digital networks are still able to shield their shows from magical distribution? Sometimes you can ONLY get your hands on a mirror, not a phone or a tablet, and why does that mean we have to timeshift the shows we ~~love obsess over~~ need like oxygen?

I will accept nothing less than a near-live viewing experience, and I'm not the only one. I'm travelling with some of the hardest of hardcore *Bromancers* fans in my life, and we all need to see that episode the second it's available (12 noon AEST Monday morning, cannot wait!) or someone's gonna get murdered.

What have your favourite eps been so far this season? I've been loving all the extra Eli/Tate feels (though you know I'm a Cinnovate shipper at heart, haha), and the road trip from hell theme pulls a lot of threads together that the show only hinted at before.

Like, we know that the bros have a soul-bond, that their magic is linked and that they are STRONGER TOGETHER, but this is the season that made this explicit, by making the soul-bond malfunction (trapping them in the demon car, oh, the glorious fanfics you darlings have wrought from this premise, I've never read so many backseat blowjobs in my life). Add to that we got that whole gorgeous flashback episode which showed us the bros meeting for the first time at the frat house — yes, their magic was soul-linked even before they were friends, I win a pie — and confirmed to fans that their magical connection is DIRECTLY CONNECTED TO MOMENTS OF HIGH EMOTION, IT'S CANON NOW, THEY CAN'T TAKE THIS AWAY FROM US.

Plus that whole time travel episode where the bros swapped bodies with the original Bromancers from the 90's, Chet and Rachel, which answered so many questions. Can girls be bros? Why yes they can! Can bros hook up romantically without losing their bromancer mojo? IT'S MESSY BUT THERE'S PRECEDENT!

While I preferred it in Season 2 when we thought Chet & Rachel were 100% platonic because there's nothing subversive or original about a straight m/f friendship developing into romance in a popular TV show, this episode was clearly signposting a potential future narrative for our bros, and the future of the show.

I'm laying my heart on the line with this one. I think the show is gonna go there. Maybe not this season — but if not now, when? There's no silver medal on offer if they pull another Teen Vamp scenario, saving the big gay romance for the final scene of the final season.

Go big or go home, *Bromancers*. We want boys kissing on TV, stat!

REFLECTION BY **MSCINNOVAR**:

Memei, what do you think of the headcanon that Chet & Rachel's romantic relationship led to the loss of their powers, which is why they were passed on to Dan & Charlie, and eventually to our own beloved bros Eli & Tate? Are the writers hinting at the idea that if our Bromancers fall in love, that means the end of the show, with them passing their powers on to a new pairing?

Or is that just an excuse to drag on the eye-fucking and the queerbaiting for another three seasons before they even start to address what the fans have seen all along? (So yeah the Teen Vemp reference might not be so far-fetched)

REFLECTION BY **MEMEI**:

Chet and Rachel's soul-link and their friendship became stronger and more powerful when they kissed. So I don't think that the 'maybe almost gay panic' moment between Eli & Tate in Ep 6 was just there for cheap laughs. They're gonna need some serious firepower to take down/save Big Bad Cinnovar in the season finale… and the demon car was taken off the board last week.

So… what else have they got in their arsenal?

Smoochytimes!

If someone spoils this episode for me before I see it because of this dratted music festival, I'm going to set fire to something. Or someone. (Not looking at the drummer who has been tapping random patterns on the back of my seat the whole drive so far,

we know you have rhythm, Sage, there's no need to keep going
on about it.)

*REFLECTION BY **KISSMETATE***:
*OMG I always forget you're friends with the actual band
members of Fake Geek Girl. I loved that song of theirs, Resting
Witch Face? It totally reminds me of my ex. Do they have a new
album coming out soon?*

REFLECTION BY **MEMEI**:
There was a new album planned for early next year, but if their
drummer keeps behaving like a kindergartener on the second leg
of our road trip he's gonna end up with no hands, so.

CHAPTER 4

HEBE IS UNEXPECTEDLY HOUSE PROUD

SATURDAY

My magic is so embarrassing.

Hallows descend from a long line of rural hedgewitches. Most of our family tree gravitated to small towns around the greener parts of the East Coast, including several adorable tourist spots around Victoria and Tasmania, the states most likely to feature English-style villages.

Our immediate family moved to the city when Holly and I were old enough for high school, but as soon as we got our university entrance confirmed, the Mums ditched the city flat and went scurrying straight back to the lavender farm in the Dandenongs where we spent our childhood. They have their own bees, and sell candles at outrageous tourist prices from a tiny shop.

Hallow magic has always skewed towards the practical. I have several cousins who run a blacksmith's forge — it's more hipster art than horse-shoeing these days, but that's where their magic finds its source, and good for them, sticking with an old school trade until it became commercially viable again. I have uncles who are butchers, bakers, tailors. Most of my aunts are doctors.

Then there's me, and Holly.

She might be an indie rock star on the rise, and I might be…
let's face it, destined for a career in admin. But when it comes to
our magic, we are, well.

We're domestic.

Holly hides it better than I do. She only cooks if it's something that's going to look amazing on Instagram. She leaves her
band clutter around our flat to disguise the fact that it's always
spotless.

I'm a gender studies major. I know there's nothing wrong
with domestic competence, but… it feels so anti-feminist, every
time my magic hums with satisfaction from making people
comfortable in our home, from cooking a meal or making a bed.

Like my magic decided that the only function I'm good for is
to be a 1950's housewife.

I won't deny that it comes in useful at times. Like when you
have to set up camp a with a horde of twenty-year-olds. Dec's
steady hands and Mei's innate understanding of tent geometry
went a long way towards being useful, but they weren't the
reason that everyone's airbeds stayed plump all night, or the ants
stayed away from our freshly-dug sandy spot, or the air of the
sleeping tents smelled faintly of lemons as we awoke for the first
full day of Winterfest.

That was all me. My magic. And it was me holding myself
back. I could have put a mimosa in each of their hands as they
crawled out to face the morning, and conjured perfect blueberry
pancakes out of the air. But I did not.

Sure, there was a pot of cinnamon apple porridge stirring
itself on a low campfire, but I'm only human. Also, that pot is a
family heirloom.

Feeding people makes me happy, shut up.

Sage was jittery and hyper. He tapped out some tune on the
leg of his jeans as he took over boiling the water for peppermint
tea.

Dec looked like death warmed up. "If I had the strength, I
would cut off your giant drumming mitts and stick them on a
flagpole," he grunted at Sage, fishing around in our supplies tent
for genuine black teabags. His natural magic levels are so low,

and so irrelevant to his sense of identity that he doesn't worry about caffeine.

"Bad night?" I said sympathetically.

Dec leaned in, hooking an elbow around my neck. "Hebes. My own, my precious Hebe, light of my life. He was tapping *all night*. I think he was drumming in his sleep. You have to do something. Save me, Hebe-wan Kenobi, you're my only hope."

"What did you have in mind?"

"Assassination?" Dec suggested hopefully

"It'll be fine," Sage insisted. "I'll have it by tonight. Just… trying to find the right beat for a new song. A new sound."

"Oh, Dec, I'm so sorry," I breathed. "Honestly. If I knew he was working on a new song, I wouldn't have let him come." Sage in creative mode was insufferable.

"Hey I am right here!" Sage called out, not sounding remotely offended. "Being a genius. You're welcome."

My left hand conjured a mimosa and pressed it against Dec's chest, almost without my conscious mind being involved in the process. "Leave it with me," I muttered. "I'll see what I can do."

Mei. Mei could share with Sage without killing him. She normally stayed awake until 3am anyway… of course, that was when she had wi-fi access. Last night she kept jerking awake every few hours to check her magic mirror, which she had bespelled to reflect the contents of her phone, despite all the glitch feedback a charm like that attracted.

It was fine. I didn't need sleep.

"You can swap with Mei tonight," I told Dec. She was still asleep in our tent, so there was no one to argue with the change of sleeping arrangements.

Dec nodded gratefully, staggered over to the campfire and started ladeling porridge into a Fake Geek Girls Know Their Shit mug. "You're an angel, Hebes. You're my general and my hero. I would kiss you if I didn't have a vengeful and suspicious girlfriend."

So this was camping with the band. Not a complete disaster so far, but then Holly hadn't dragged home a new boyfriend yet. The weekend was still young.

Speaking of my twin sister, there she was now, walk-of-no-shaming her way up the path to our sheltered spot, wearing yesterday's clothes. Her hair was a bird's nest, her shirt was barely buttoned, and those were not her shoes.

Her makeup was perfect. Domestic magic strikes again.

"I'm in love!" she announced, helping herself to peppermint tea.

"I'm gonna need coffee for this," grumbled Sage. "Do we have to pretend we like whatever Dave Matthews loving douchecanoe you've decided to latch on to this weekend? Or can we skip that part and go straight to convincing you to break up with him?"

"You're tragic and no one wants to sleep with you," Holly said sweetly. "I didn't mean a person, Sage. Last night changed my life. I found a sound. The new sound we need, to take Fake Geek Girl to the next level."

Sage's hand paused, hovering in the middle of the pattern he was tapping out on his own mug. "Yeah?"

"Yeah," said Holly. They exchanged a look, a fierce mutual love of their band and their music and everything they had in common.

If they were remotely attracted to each other, they would have burned the world down in the flame of their love story. But they weren't that, had never been that.

It still felt like the rest of us might get scorched if we got too close to Sage and Holly when they had those looks on their faces.

"Ugh," said Dec into his porridge. "If you two are gonna be brilliant and inspiring at each other, I'm going back to bed."

"Rack off then," said Holly, helping herself to breakfast. "Is Juniper up yet? I need to update her on all the awesomeness she flaked out on last night."

"So much for taking her with you as a guarantee of good behaviour," I said pointedly.

"Wow. Careful, Hebes, your middle-aged governess is show-ing." Holly tasted the mug, made a face (obviously hating how perfectly the porridge was seasoned) and wandered over to the tent she had been supposed to sleep in last night. "Junie, are you decent? I'm coming in." She unzipped it, then backed away, looking worried. "Huh."

"What's up?" asked Dec.

"I guess Juniper didn't come home last night either."

"Get it, Juniper," said Sage, impressed.

I caught the hesitation in her voice. "Where exactly did you leave her? Holly?"

"It's fine," said Holly. "I'm sure it's fine."

My magic, which had been so happy and content when I thought everyone was comfortable and looked-after, gave an uncomfortable lurch.

Where had Juniper spent the night?

CHAPTER 5

WHATEVER HAPPENED TO MISS JUNIPER CRESSWELL, GENTLEWOMAN AND CELLIST?

DEAR DIARY

I don't do this. I'm not like this. Last night was an anomaly.
That's a lie.

A lot of what happened last night was out of character, but I
can't say it was an anomaly. I followed Holly Hallow, and
shenanigans ensued. That pretty much sums up the pattern of
everything I've done since she and her enchanted flyers entered
my life.

Holly Hallow does something crazy, and I follow her.

———

THERE ARE times when I question my place in an indie rock
band. I'm a classically trained musician. Twelve of my closest
relatives including both parents, four aunts and uncles, my
grandfather and several cousins, each play for one the country's
three premier orchestras: the Sydney Siren Chamber Orchestra,
the Floating Orchestra in Melbourne, or the Tasmanian
Symphony Orchestra. My parents were expecting me to major in
Real Music, with a possible minor in Unreal Music, as part of an
ongoing path that has been mapped out for me since I was six
years old.

Me + professional cello-playing destiny = true happiness.

But when I started at Belladonna U, staring at that whole curriculum of formalised music study, I couldn't do it. I was done. Burned out. I fled to Unreal Humanities.

My parents had the expected collective meltdown, even when I promised them I was majoring in Political Science, that I wasn't completely immersing myself in an indulgence of nineteenth century literature (my one true love).

They couldn't understand me giving up music.

Truthfully, I only gave it up for a month. Four quiet weeks, before I followed a pretty girl who was stapling flyers to bulletin boards across campus. The flyers sang at you when you got near them, and there was something about the lyrics, so silly and geeky and fun.

It was so long since music had been fun for me.

My parents tried not to look smug and say "We told you so" when I went home for the weekend and collected Irene, my cello.

Needless to say, they were not delighted to discover that I wanted Irene with me to audition for an odd little geek rock band instead of fulfilling the orchestral destiny they had planned for me.

———

THAT WAS MORE than two years ago, and I have learned to trust myself. Following Holly Hallow into adventure and shenanigans is worth it, every time.

It's not just because she's so pretty it makes my heart hurt.

It's not just because she's fierce in a way that women simply aren't, in my family.

It's mostly because the adventures she leads me on are more than I would ever find for myself.

FRIDAY NIGHT

Following Holly was my first mistake. Losing her was my second.

"Just one drink," I heard her promising Hebe, who wasn't impressed we were decamping so early. "I'll take Juniper with me." Holly was using her most innocent voice.

She was also clearly using me.

Hebe gave her twin a dirty look, not fooled at all. "Juniper's presence does not guarantee your good behaviour."

"You know you're not actually my mother, right?"

I cleared my throat. "Holly, I'm thirsty."

Hebe gave me an impatient look, and washed her hands of both of us. "Fine. Try not to pick fights with any band you want to open for someday."

"That leaves so many options," Holly grinned.

"No it does not," Hebe said sternly.

———————

WITCHES DON'T LIKE to rough it. Sure, we were living in tents for a few days, but that didn't mean we couldn't do it in style.

The drinking tents at Winterfest were works of art. They looked like canvas on the outside, but once you stepped inside, you found yourself in a world of wonder and aesthetic glory.

Holly and I drank ouzo in an Athenian amphitheatre, champagne in a Parisian cabaret/karaoke bar, and something that I'm pretty sure was absinthe in a grimy Parisian night-den that looked from the outside like a Dryzabone propped up on three sticks, but had room inside for three chandeliers and several ornate fainting couches.

Holly likes to get the lay of the land, the first night at any music festival. She knows four times as many people as I do, but she never lets a conversation last for longer than five minutes. She always wants to be the first person to develop Opinions on which hangouts are best, and which are best avoided. That requires research.

With music festivals, everything's a performance. Where ever you go, someone is singing or playing or unofficially auditioning for someone else's band.

Holly was drawing more of a crowd than usual, and by the time the eighth person casually dropped into conversation that they had keyboarding experience, I finally twigged what was going on.

"Are we looking for a new band member?" I hissed in her ear.

"No," she said, laughing it off. "Of course not."

"Why does everyone think we are?"

She looked shifty. "I might have sent out some feelers?"

"You didn't think to talk it over with Sage and I first?"

Holly shrugged, guiltless as ever. "We all know the band's been spinning its wheels since Nora ditched us. Sage and I have talked about it a few times. He thinks we need a new sound — different songs, moving forward with the music. *I* think we need another person. If I find the right one he'll come around soon enough."

"Oh." That stung. Of course Holly and Sage had talked about what the band needed — or argued about it, whatever. They were like cats in a sack, those two, always scratching at each other, but they were close in a way they'd never been with me. Fake Geek Girl was theirs first, before they added Nora and me.

Would they even notice if Irene and I disappeared from the band? Would they miss me the way we all miss Nora? How long would it take before they replaced me with some new sound?

We were between our fourth and fifth drinking tents when Holly heard the voice. "That's it," she said, ditching her cider bottle in a nearby recycling zone and hurrying away from the fairy lights of the designated paths.

"What's what?"

"The sound, Junie, the thing we've been missing. That's it. That's her."

She followed the voice. And of course, I followed her. It's what I do.

———

LET me condense our adventures somewhat. In search of the perfect voice who would apparently serve as some sort of musical bandaid to repair the undefinable missing something in our band, Holly Hallow and I may or may not have done the following:

- 1) tripped over three stoned *Bromancers* fans arguing about whether or not the season finale was going to be a game changer.
- 2) strayed into the camping ground of the Metal Headed Wombats, territory we usually stay clear of because Sage hooked up with 3 of the 4 band-members three festivals ago (yes, all on the same weekend) and the fallout almost destroyed their band.
- 3) discovered there was a secret knitting community on site, which does not take kindly to random visitors. Knitters are territorial.
- 4) accidentally set off several privacy proximity charms, which led to the unexpected revelation that two Actually Quite Famous members of different bands who are both married to Actually Quite Famous other people were sharing a tent while naked, along with a third Actually Quite Famous solo act. Oops. Sorry.
- 5) Hid in a bush to eavesdrop on a private beach party including the crooning, husky voice of a siren with laugh-lines and tie-dyed jeans.

Who happened to be my Lit Professor. So. That was a thing. Prof Nettle normally wore librarian-chic tweed, her hair in a messy bun, and the most sensible shoes known to witchkind.

Tonight she was barefoot, a guitar resting on her knees, and a crowd of adoring fans circled around her as she sang a cheesy old Betty Hubble cover, with folksy sass and surprising depth.

"That's her," Holly breathed. "That's the voice I heard

earlier. She's a MILF and a half."

I elbowed her hard. "Hol, we have to go." I couldn't be here. Couldn't be involved with this. Professor Nettle looked all soft around the edges here on the sands, but she was notoriously sharp-edged and scathing in the classroom. I'd taken several of her classes without her ever paying the slightest bit of attention to me, and that was exactly how I liked it.

"I want to talk to her. She's gorgeous. And that voice…"

"Holly," I hissed. "You can't have her."

Telling Holly Hallow she can't have something is like telling a cakeoholic that they should save the last slice for tomorrow.

"Come on," she said urgently, and scrambled through the bush, in search of the professor with the killer voice.

I stepped away, pulling back from her.

It's not like I expected her to follow me. That's not our pattern. But I waited ten minutes, anyway, before I decided to head back on my own.

———

THAT WAS when the evening went really wrong. I didn't remember the way back to the safe 'lighted path' zone, which left me wandering around in the dark.

I found one thread of fairy lights, only to realise that they were will o' the wisps and not genuine helpful fairies, which led me back to a different stretch of the beach, nowhere near the camping equivalent of civilisation.

I hate that I do this. I let Holly drag me around until I'm no longer convenient. Every single time.

I hate that when she's paying attention to me, I'd rather be with her than anywhere else. So much for self-respect.

Finally, I found a sign saying LOST WITCHES, THIS WAY TO THE PARTEEE, with a large arrow pointing back over the dunes. I scrambled up and over, finding myself on a path with genuine fairy lights, then zeroed in on a charmed map of the full campsite with a sigh of relief. If I went via the Hobbit pub and the history tent, it wouldn't take me long at all.

And if Holly's antics were anything to go by, I'd have the tent to myself tonight.

"Hey," said a cheerful voice. "Aren't you Juniper Cresswell? I love Fake Geek Girl. Like, you're my favourite band of all time."

I never get recognised. Not unless I have Irene with me, and sometimes not even then.

The group is a little bit famous, in some circles. I don't mind that. It's like an orchestra — we're all part of something bigger than the sum of its parts. I wear makeup on the YouTube vids so I look different to the real life version of me. It's always Sage or Holly on the publicity materials, or a distant shot of the three of us, because I hate it when people pay attention to me.

Still, politeness costs nothing.

"Thanks," I said, turned and smiled towards the owner of the voice. She was cute, in a bright homemade Save Cinnovate shirt, with bright teal curls under a knitted beanie. "Have you seen us at Medea's Cauldron?"

"Only on YouTube," said the adorable fangirl. "I'm so excited for your set here, though. Sunday, right?"

"Sunday," I confirmed. "On Stage 4, early evening."

"I'll be there," said the cutie. "Holly Hallow is so hot. I don't know how you can stand to be near her all the time."

Ha, tell me about it.

"Can I hug you?" she asked, already lurching in my direction.

No! "Um, sure?"

The fangirl flung her arms around me, surrounding me with the thick scent of cloves and lavender and a thick tang of — frankincense?

A warning siren went off in my head, because I knew those ingredients, that was basic spellcraft and… something sharp stung the back of my neck, before I could yank myself away.

"Sorry," said the fangirl as her face went misty in front of me, and then disappeared into blackness. "But really. I wouldn't do this if it wasn't like, mega-important. It's for the good of the band."

CHAPTER 6

SAGE TO THE RESCUE

SATURDAY

WE HADN'T EVEN BEEN at Winterfest for a full day, and we'd already lost our cellist. Hebes was freaking out, and Holly was pretending not to care, which only made Hebe more frantic but also pissed off.

Dec and Mei made themselves scarce, claiming they were forming a search party. Yeah, right.

My magic sparked up, reacting to the tension that rolled off the girls. "Hey, Hebes," I interrupted. "I'm gonna go see if I can spot her from the air."

She threw a teacup at me.

Which was impressive because, I don't think there was a single teacup in the camp. Not like this one, not proper pink china with roses and a saucer. Hebe's magic is chill most of the time, but home furnishings sometimes appear around her when she's upset. I was prepared to take a cup to the face but Hebe froze it before it collided with my nose. She looked horrified. "Sage, I'm sorry."

"No big. I'm gonna…" Yeah, Mei and Dec had the right idea. Up up and away.

I'VE HAD the same broomstick for years. It's sturdy and workmanlike, not one of the fancier models out there. Good old basic stick with bristles. He and I have been through some shit together, and when I need to pour off excess energy, Bruce is there to help a bloke out.

Yeah, my broom is called Bruce, what of it?

First time I came to Winterfest, I was fifteen but big for my age and I signed up as a volunteer to get the discount. They had me on security and I learned a lot about how it all works behind the scenes.

Everyone assumes that the whole 'no wi-fi' policy is a hipster thing, to force us all to enjoy the music in the moment instead of live-tweeting it, or whatever. That, and Winterfest prides itself on magical display and pyroenchantments during the night shows. When you have planned your events around that much volatile magic, you need to dial down on the Unreal tech.

That's all true. But the inside word I got during my security gig is that there's a bunch of curseware webbed into the Winterfest infrastructure to prevent certain spells from being cast. Keeping that curseware stable is the main reason they block not only wi-fi but all internet and phone signals from Mandrake Sands at this time of year.

Location charms are on the official blocked and banned list. A lot of big name celebs come to Winterfest. Tradition has them mucking in with the rest of us, but they have legit safety and privacy concerns. Location spells make it really easy for stalkers and journos to get way too much information about how to zero in on the festival's Big Name Performers.

Mei and Dec weren't going to have much luck finding Juniper using magic.

I knew the weak spots in the system. Like, the curse field that kept out all the Unapproved Enchantments and Internet Juice? If you flew high enough, you could get clear of the field.

Four hundred feet above the campsite, with a broom gripped

between my thighs, I cast the location charm. It spun out of me, glazing the world violet for a moment. I concentrated all my thoughts on my mate Juniper: her soft smile, her obsession with dead white lady authors, her brightly blazing crush on Holly (the one thing we never joked about because it had dragged on way too long to be anything but awkward).

Juniper.

I saw a spark beneath me, and sent a thought spinning out across the campsite. *Hebe.*

She got back to me straight away, huffing with impatience. *What's the rule about telepathy, Sage?*

Boyfriends and sisters only, I know, and they have to apply in writing three days ahead of time. I still need you to look at a map of the site, facing north.

She huffed again. Hebe was the only person I knew who could do that inside her head. *Hang on. There's one not far from... yep, here it is.*

I breathed. *Okay, follow the fairy lights path south of Stage 3, on the west side. Got it?*

Hating it.

Four tents down from there, a roundish one on the east of that path. There's some kind of... tree line?

Huh, said Hebe. *I think that's the Tim Tam Slam Club.*

The what?

It's like, a cabaret karaoke bar? Holly listed it as one of the places she and Juniper went last night.

Juniper's there now.

Meet you there, Hebe thought briskly at me.

GOOD THING I had the directions, because the location spell vanished as I flew lower, and it was hard to tell one big tent from another, the closer I got. I landed near Stage 3, banging my knee awkwardly on one of the humming anti-wifi markers.

Something Wicked were playing. Muffling spells had been set around the back of the stage so that the sound of the band only carried forward, but I'd know those vibrations in my sleep. Bloody hell, I hadn't wanted to miss them, they finally had their original drummer back.

There's this law of music festivals: you never get to see the acts you went there for, and the faves you do make it to always have a bad set or a tech failure. The best music at a festival comes from the bands you weren't expecting to enjoy, and didn't plan to bother seeing.

So yeah, here was me limping off to something called the Tim Tam Slam Club instead of hanging around to hear one of my favourite indie bands play live, whatever.

I found Juniper almost immediately. She… really didn't need to be rescued. She was sitting on the bar, crooning into a microphone, cuddling a girl in a blonde ponytail who… well. Who looked a lot like Holly. I'd seen Holly wear that exact outfit on stage, the tiny silver dress, the giant fluffy ugg boots and the denim replica jacket from *The Bromancers* with Cinnovar's name spelled out on the back in fake sigils.

(Holly didn't actually know what she was wearing when she stole that jacket from Mei, she just thought it was cool, and after fans started tweeting her about how awesome it was, she ordered her own)

Juniper and her new friend were singing Judy Garland karaoke, which was a whole lot more retro than I had any patience for.

An odd look crossed Juniper's face when she saw me, like she couldn't believe I was here. Then she hiccupped, "SAGE!" and practically threw herself across the bar to hug me.

This was new. Juniper wasn't the touchy-feely type. Not with me, anyway. I patted her head awkwardly. "You okay? We were worried you didn't come back to camp last night."

She tipped her face up to mine, glowing. "I have been having the *best time*."

"Are you drunk?" I asked.

"We had breakfast mohitos," she said with a giggle. That was off, too. I don't think I'd ever heard Juniper giggle before.

Maybe this was good. She was making other friends, cutting

loose a little. I might be a big brother type to every girl in our band but that didn't mean I had the right to get all protective and shit. Had to trust them to set their own limits.

"Just," I said. "You gotta check in, babe. Every now and then, so we know you're okay."

Juniper booped me on the nose. "You called me babe!" She giggled again.

"We'll look after her," said Blonde Ponytail Holly Replica, giving me a stern look. She came up and hooked her arm in Juniper's. "She's awesome."

"Sure, I know that. Pace yourself, yeah?" I added to Juniper. "Maybe eat something solid? And we need you for rehearsal tomorrow morning. Ten AM, back at camp."

"Ten AM," Juniper nodded, giving me a wobbly salute. "Because we play tomorrow." Her eyes glowed with delight. "I get to play Irene on stage!"

"Yep," I agreed. "She's missing you. Don't neglect her too long." I was such a grown up right now. Was this what Hebe felt like when we treated her like the band mum, here to put band-aids on our ouchies and make us soothing cups of tea?

"You can stay if you like, Sage," said the not-Holly, giving me a very pointed once-over. "We have more drinks coming."

Not even lunchtime. Wow, where did that come from? When did I become the judgy old man of this band?

"Some other time," I said, then collected a dainty fistbump from Juniper and backed out of her space.

"That seems out of character," said a low voice as I left the tent.

Ferd was hanging out by the entrance, a formal silk jacket over his shirt and jeans, plus boots that were way too nice for the muddy paths around here.

"Shit that happens at Winterfest stays at Winterfest," I said automatically, then did a double take. "Hey, man."

"Hey," said Ferd. We did a bro arm-clasp thing because we hadn't seen each other for like, a day.

"I thought you weren't coming," I said warily. If Ferd was here… nah. Jules Nightshade wouldn't be seen dead in a henna-hippie-hellscape of live music and mung beans like Mandrake Sands.

Besides, we'd broken up. It usually took him at least three days to sulk and recover before he came back to get his flirt on.

"We changed our minds," said Ferd. "Thought I'd surprise Hebe."

"Mate," I said, smacking him firmly on the shoulder. "*Mate*. You've known Hebes for like, half a year now. How do you not know that she *really* hates surprises?"

CHAPTER 7

MEI MAKES A LIST

SATURDAY

> You Are Gazing Into the Mirror of **MeMei**
> Who Is… **high on caffeine & indie music.**
> **Camping is still the worst.**
> *Add Your Reflections Below!*

DAY 1 OF WINTERFEST, By the Numbers!

- Mugs of porridge consumed: 4
- Cups of coffee/chocolate purchased from a food truck: 6.
- (It would have been 2 but the barista kind of looks like Edward Scissorhands & I kept going back to see if I could get him to smile.)
- Number of smiles encouraged out of the Edward Scissorhands barista: 0.5
- Favourite bands spotted: 12 if you include partial spottings such as Cally from the Misers in line for coffee and Benedict from Charmed Life making the long trek to the 'nicotine friendly zone' which, by all

accounts, is so far from the main camping grounds
that it's practically in Brisbane.

- Favourite performance: OK I was technically
  supposed to be looking for a missing camping buddy
  (who turned out to be totes not missing, hooray) but I
  managed to catch half of Something Wicked's set and
  it was off the charts good. Their cover of Halo was
  surprising but worked really well, and I loved both
  songs from their new album Ancient Alchemy. The
  new drummer is supes hot btw.

- Conversations about *The Bromancers*: about 47, I'll
  admit it, I lost count. But I am making so many
  awesome new friends just by asking people what
  their weirdest, most batshit strange predictions are for
  the finale. Y'all have some very vivid imaginations!

- Camping dramahs: at least 7. Mostly caused by
  unexpected guests turning up at our site and… well,
  making their presence known in all kinds of fun
  ways. I'm staying out of it. My lips are sealed.

- Progress on getting past the wi-fi free zone to score
  access to a certain TV episode: 0 for now. Watch this
  space.

- Favours traded in the hopes that one of them will
  develop into a definite lead on solving the
  Bromancers dilemma: so many. So many favours.
  But it will all come good in the end.

- Right?

CHAPTER 8

HEBE AND THE VERY BIG, COMPLETELY FINE NO BIG DEAL

SATURDAY

ON THE BRIGHT SIDE, Juniper wasn't missing any more, according to the mirror message that Sage swiped in my direction before haring off towards a beer or a bass player or whatever else was distracting him right now.

Juniper was not dead in a ditch. That was good.

On the… completely also bright side, my boyfriend had unexpectedly arrived at Winterfest. Despite me repeatedly checking that this wasn't something he planned to do.

Surprises are romantic, apparently.

"Didn't you have plans with your parents today?" I asked, still trying to catch up with these new developments.

"Yeah that's not a thing any more," Ferd said quickly. "No big deal."

Does anyone ever say no big deal when a thing is really no big deal? I opened my mouth to push further on the whole 'no big deal' question, then I realised I hadn't kissed him yet, and did that instead.

Kissing him was nice, even if my mind was already spinning forward into the logistics of sleeping arrangements… oh hell. "Are Viola and Jules here too?" I asked, very casually. No big deal.

"Yep, they're excited to see the bands," said Ferd. "Now I know this is a hassle for you…"

"Oh no," I started to say, because it was that or grabbing him by the collar to howl: WHY DIDN'T YOU SAY YOU WERE COMING SO I COULD PLAN FOR IT?

"…But I promise we won't mess up your camping game plan or anything. We won't be any extra trouble. It's all sorted."

That was… ominous.

"When you say all sorted," I started to say.

"Like, I told them you had this whole plan and we weren't factored into it, so we're going to have to look after ourselves."

"And when you say look after yourselves you mean… staying at a nearby hotel?" The thought of Jules Nightshade and Viola Vale attempting to camp brought me out in hives. They did know that camping happened outdoors, didn't they? Why were they even here?

"No, they're back at the campsite. Setting up our gear. I promise, you don't have to worry about a thing." He kissed the top of my head. "Want to go pick a band to watch? Who's on this afternoon?"

"I think," I said slowly. "I think I want to just pop back to the campsite and check everything's…"

"No," Ferd said too quickly. "I mean, we have this whole plan. So we don't make any extra work for you."

"I was heading back there anyway. I tapped my hand-mirror and shoved it in a pocket. "Juniper crisis averted, so. That's where I'm going."

"Sure," said my boyfriend, looking uncomfortable. "Just do what you were gonna do. I won't get in your way."

I tried not to break into a run as we headed back to camp.

———

IT EVEN SMELLED DIFFERENT. My magic whimpered to me as I approached the campsite. My calm, simple, low key campsite.

There was a large rolled-up carpet leaning against a gorse bush as we headed up the path. It smelled of wealth, privilege and antique flying charms, musty like they'd stolen it from a museum.

"We may have made a few improvements," Ferd called apologetically from behind me.

Colour burst across my eyeballs as I stepped into our cozy bush clearing.

Where we had previously had 3 large tents and 1 small tent set up in a semi-circle around the fire pit, plus a large tarpaulined area for beanbag lounging which could be quickly cleared away for band practice...

Well, now there were two extra tents, bright green and so brand new that they squeaked. There was also a... pavilion was the only word for it. Draped with Indian silks, it exploded in colour, comfort and decadence. Warmth rolled off it, with a spicy scent that suggested protection and relaxation enchantments. Giant pillows spilled out, on to the ground which was... apparently tiled now. In marble.

Dec lay sprawled on the cushions with a very animated Viola Vale lying half on top of him, chatting lazily. Their relationship made no sense to me. Apparently his type was 'smart and spiky' while hers was... super chill gamer geek?

Mei was perched in one of several brand new canvas chairs, the kind that fold up so small with one containment rune that they can fit in your pocket. She was buried a mirror chat, too distracted to look up.

Jules Nightshade sat at my campfire, feet on a stool, looking proud of himself. He was eating some kind of panini, which clearly came from the silver "five minute meal" cauldron that hung over our campfire, having displaced my family's enchanted porridge pot (now sitting forlornly on the sidelines).

"We may have gone overboard," said Ferd behind me.

"It all looks very comfortable," I said, which was true. They had done a great job of accommodating themselves. I should be pleased.

The trouble with domestic magic — and this is another embarrassing revelation — is that it's inherently competitive. It doesn't just want the people around it to be comfortable and well looked after. It wants to be the one responsible for that.

I'd indulged my magic in setting up camp for the band — something I rarely did, and now it was awake and howling about how Jules bloody Nightshade had wandered in with his endless budget and glamorous tastes, and changed everything. It wasn't mine any more.

It's possible I have a domestic magic problem.

That wasn't Ferd's fault. It wasn't even Jules and Viola's fault. They'd tried to be helpful. They hadn't done anything wrong. It was no big deal — it *should* be no big deal.

I turned to smile at him, to say how nice it all was, to smooth over the horrible feeling that I wanted to burst into tears.

Luckily for me, Holly interrupted. Thank goodness for her terrible sense of timing. "Hebe, we have a big freaking problem with Juniper!"

———

"I STILL DON'T SEE the problem," I said, fifteen minutes later. Ferd had been remarkably understandable that I had to go with Holly and her crisis, because that was what I was here for. We'd catch up later.

I almost certainly wasn't avoiding him, now that he was here.

What I hadn't expected was that Holly's crisis was actually… well, a crisis. She was freaking out, and I hadn't yet managed to nail down exactly why.

"I don't see how you can queue for coffee like a normal person when Juniper is clearly under some kind of evil curse," Holly hissed at me, joggling up and down as we waited in line at the Cirque De Cacao beverage truck. "Possibly she offended a fairy. These things happen *all the time*."

"I need coffee," I said in a calm, steady voice. "Because otherwise my magic is going to break up with my boyfriend."

"Oh." She hesitated and looked closer at me. "Crap. The Basilisk Brats kind of messed up your campsite, didn't they?"

"It's no big deal," I said between gritted teeth.

"Why don't you explain to Ferd that your magic is an epic Housewitch Magazine control freak that needs to be in charge of everyone else's comfort?"

"Or I could drink a double latte and get over myself. Double latte, please," I added to Evan, the nice goth barista who was manning the truck today.

"Hey, Evan," said Holly, her attention still on me.

"Hey, Holly," said the barista, and frothed some milk quickly to cover up the fact that while we were equal regulars at the bricks and mortar version of Cirque De Cacao, Holly's was the only name he remembered.

That's not unusual for us.

"Decaf?" he asked, in case I wanted to roll back my order.

"Nope," I said grimly.

"I've got a couple of orders queued up, it will be about three minutes."

"I'll have a cinnamon choc froth," Holly told him, and dragged me aside. "Can you pause your drama while I tell you about mine?"

"Wow. I think that's the first time you've ever asked me that instead of bulldozing through regardless."

"Cute. So Juniper is not acting like herself. Ever since she went missing, she's been… off."

"You mean since you ditched her to flirt with an attractive older lady with a guitar?"

"The love of my life, yes. Seriously, Hebe. I tried to talk to Junie just now, and she completely brushed me off to go listen to Charmed Life with some OTHER GIRL."

I looked at Holly, patiently.

She had finished her argument. Her eyes were wide, and her hands were… expressive.

"I'm glad she's making new friends," I said finally.

"Is that all you have to say? There's something wrong, Hebe. Juniper never acts like that around me. She wasn't acting like… like Juniper."

"So she stopped letting you take her for granted and treat her like a doormat for five seconds, and you think she's under a curse?" I snapped.

Holly looked like I had slapped her. "That's not fair."

"It's not inaccurate."

"Cinnamon choc froth for Holly," Evan called out from the beverage truck. "And, uh, double actual caffeine latte?"

I stomped over to the truck, paid for both drinks, and started downing my latte before I even handed Holly her cup of chocolate. The itchy discomfort that had been clawing at me since I realised what Jules Nightshade and the others had done to my campsite finally, finally began to ebb.

"I know I'm right," Holly said softly, beside me.

"So fix it," I told her. "It's not always my job to fix things. Take some initiative."

It was nothing. Obviously it was nothing. Genuinely no big deal. But it wouldn't hurt Holly to focus on someone other than herself for ten minutes.

Brace yourself, Juniper. Holly's coming to save you.

CHAPTER 9

THE SECRET DIARY OF MISS JUNIPER CRESSWELL, UNDER NEW MANAGEMENT

FRIDAY

DEAR DIARY

This isn't the first time that I have had my body stolen, or possessed, or enchanted to obey a will other than my own. This isn't even the third time.

My family's magical affinity with music has led to some rather strange incidents over the years. My eldest sister is a banshee, my younger sister a siren. Before the decade of vocal training it took them both to control their powers, I was stuck in the middle.

Carmen stole my voice once, for a whole year. She meant to do it, but didn't realise how hard it would be to give it back once she was caught.

Calypso used to hum enchantments at me if she couldn't be bothered to get out of bed for breakfast. I would stand against my own volition, march into the kitchen, make cereal and apple slices, and return to the bedroom with a tray.

I fought it, at first, deliberately jolting or tipping the tray, so that her bed ended up a mess and she got the blame. But that only encouraged her to practice so that she could increase her control.

She developed the skill to the point that she could force me to get out of bed and make her breakfast without actually waking me up.

It sounds horrific but honestly, most childhoods have stories like that in them, don't they? Maybe not of the misuse of magic, but some form of bullying or manipulation among the siblings. I had the reputation as the nice one, the sweet one, and I used that to my advantage — I never took revenge every single time that Carm or Caly did something wicked to me, but I saved it up. When I enacted my vengeances, I timed them well so that no one could accuse me without looking like they were making it up.

Both my sisters are perfectly lovely now. Carmen is second clarinet of the Floating Orchestra, and Caly is in Grade 12 at the Willows Academy, applying to Belladonna U for next year.

We almost never torment each other any more, magically or otherwise.

I should thank them, really. Because when the cute little fangirl in the Cinnovate t-shirt and the knitted beanie stole my body, my first thought was resigned familiarity.

Oh. This again.

It wasn't a traditional body swap — I'd been through one of those, too, the summer that Carmen was so angry at being sent to Woodwind Camp that she harnessed some seriously dark magic. It lasted a week, and because I was loyal I covered for her until she got sprung trying to take my fourteen year old body to a 16+ concert with her then boyfriend.

Is it any wonder I spent most of my teens preferring to hang out with Jane Austen?

Anyway. I knew that feeling of waking up in someone else's limbs, and this wasn't that. I was still resident in my body. I was just… removed from the action, observing as the fangirl took over the driving seat.

Her own body fell limply to the path. She used my voice to summon her friend Ellie L — my thief was, it turned out, called Ellie K — and between them, they carried original Ellie K to their campsite, as if she were merely drunk, and not unconscious.

No, unconscious isn't the word. *Empty.*

———

SATURDAY

They were fans. That much was obvious. This was a joyride, and all I had to do was hang on tight and hope they got bored before they crashed the vehicle.

The Ellies got drunk and giggly, watched a bunch of concerts together, and then finally got up the nerve to hang out with my bandmates at the camp on Saturday night.

No one noticed that I wasn't myself. Ellie K had clearly done her homework. On the rare occasions that the conversation opened in my direction, Ellie said something random about Jane Austen or cello music, or just smiled and gave off some pleasantry.

Apparently with the right six sound bites, I could be replaced entirely.

I had high hopes for Hebe, who was the one most likely to notice issues generally, but she was clearly rattled by the presence of the Basilisk Boyfriend Crew, and so busy pretending she didn't mind that she couldn't see anything else.

Ellie L, not restricted by having to pretend to be me, stared openly at everyone with fannish glee. She kept up a whispered commentary into my ear, and genuinely squealed when Sage and Holly started noodling around with some new song he was breaking in, even though they blew up into an argument halfway through because something about lyric scansion?

"Fine, I'll play it with Juniper," Holly huffed. She gave me a searching, challenging look. She'd been giving me a lot of those looks all day, like she was unhappy with me, like she didn't trust me… it made me feel sick and stressed, more so even than the unwanted passenger in my body.

But then Holly marched over to our tent, manhandled Irene towards me, and held her towards the wrong side of my body. She knew I hated anyone to touch Irene. She knew that wasn't how…

Oh. Holly knew.

This was a *test*.

All those glances of suspicion and dislike, they were for the passenger, not me.

To her credit, Ellie K rallied hard. "I could have done that," she protested quietly, eyes on the ground like she was embarrassed to point out Holly's poor manners.

Yes, that was a little too accurate for my liking.

"Give us that beat you've been torturing us with, Sage," Holly called out.

He tapped the beat and started to sing his rough lyrics, not quite there. Holly joined in, singing along.

I played.

Ellie K played me like I was Irene. She was an actual cellist, it turned out. No wonder she picked me as the Fake Geek Girl band member to hijack.

I realised then how much I had been hoping that Ellie K would show herself up in rehearsal, or during our set tomorrow, and that the band would finally realise something was wrong.

Instead, I saw Holly's eyes soften as Ellie K played. Like she wasn't sure whether to trust her own suspicious thoughts any more. Like maybe she had been mistaken.

I wanted to howl, "You see me! Don't give up now!"

But Holly was smiling with what looked like relief, and Ellie K was so proud of herself that her entire identity swamped mine with confidence.

I drifted deeper, losing my senses, drowning in my own body.

It went foggy. I think I slept.

———

SUNDAY

When I awoke I was in the tent, with Holly in the sleeping bag beside me, and I knew I had lost her. She wouldn't be asleep if she didn't trust that this was me and not some intruder.

———

Next time I struggled up out of the fog, Fake Geek Girl were in the middle of band practice. Ellie K kept up fine with what was expected of Juniper — she played our songs like she'd been practicing them for years, which wasn't overly surprising.

Her friend, Ellie L, sat nearby, legs swinging as she watched us. Her eyes were on Holly. She didn't look as aggressive as before. She looked contemplative, like she was measuring Holly for a new outfit…

Oh. No.

It wasn't only me I had to worry about.

Ellie L was planning to hijack a Fake Geek Girl bandmember too. Did they have another friend who had aspirations to be a drummer?

They were stealing the whole band.

From here, there was nothing I could do to stop them.

CHAPTER 10

SAGE CAN'T SOLVE ALL HIS PROBLEMS WITH COFFEE

SUNDAY

ON SUNDAY, it rained. Which pretty much put the cherry on the top of this total whipped cream disaster of a weekend.

Our whole gang was either loved up, on edge or both. Hebe was still pretending she didn't mind the Basilisk Invasion, downing so many lattes that caffeine rolled out of her pores. She was all over Ferd like she had something to prove, and he was romancing her so hard he almost strained a shoulder muscle.

Then there was Jules bloody Nightshade, posing his way around the shiny new renovated campsite like he was a VIP. I'd never seen him on his best behaviour before. He didn't turn up his nose at the food, the company or the accommodations (which, admittedly were a whole lot more swank thanks to his contribution).

When Ferd was around, Nightshade stuck to him like glue, all snark and laughter. When Ferd was making out with Hebe or disappearing into a tent with her, which happened every time one of them wanted to avoid making conversation (so all the freaking time), Nightshade would make conversation with everyone else, making so much effort I suspected he was trying to win a bet.

He sizzled with energy, like a lightning bolt in a silk dressing gown. It hurt to look at him. He didn't look at me, or acknowledge my existence, for most of the weekend.

It didn't bother me. What did I care?

Juniper finally returned to our campsite last night but brought her new friend with her. They spent all their time cuddled up together, eyeing off the rest of us like they shared a secret we weren't in on.

The song I hadn't been able to find? It itched at my skin, tapped on my rib cage, twisted my stomach. I hadn't slept in the tent I was now sharing with Mei, even after the glow of her mirror finally faded at 3am.

Don't ask me how she always looks fresh as a daisy on four hours sleep. That at least was business as usual.

"You look like crap," Mei said, perfectly awake at 7am, as if someone had plugged her into a charger and she'd just hit 100%. "Let's get breakfast somewhere that isn't here."

"That's the best suggestion anyone has made all weekend." I changed my shirt before we left the tent. If she could make an effort, so could I.

No one else was awake as we staggered out of the Fake Geek Girl campsite and into the Sunday morning drizzle. Waterproofing charms had kept the rain off the tents and our instruments during the night, but we'd need more than that if we were going to practice (and perform) in the open air.

"Worry about it later," Mei said impatiently.

Don't ask me how she wields so much authority while wearing an Athena Owl hand-knitted beanie. Some things are meant to be a mystery.

———

WE ATE bacon sandwiches in a cafe that looked like a circus tent and, unlike nearly every other commercial tent around here, was exactly the same on the inside as out.

The provider of the bacon sandwiches was comfortingly null, which meant I didn't have to drown the usual acid tang of someone else's magic in a shitload of tomato sauce for once in my life. "We should eat here all the time," I said with my mouth full.

Mei was looking at me very calmly. "So, Sage."

This couldn't be good. She was making actual eye contact. Usually you could rely on Mei to avoid social conventions. "Mei."

"You remember that episode back in the frat boy feels season, when Eli guesses that Tate is bisexual and tries to prove what an open-minded wingman he is by setting him up with all these pretty dudes, but they all turn out to be demons?"

"Yeah," I said warily, because who wouldn't remember that episode of *The Bromancers*? Clearly it was a trap, but I couldn't see the wires yet.

Mei raised her eyebrows. "You have demon makeout hang-over face."

I glowered at her. "I haven't been making out with — also hey! Nightshade is slightly evil but that doesn't make him a demon."

"Did I say anything about Nightshade?"

Man she was worse than Holly when she got going. "I haven't been making out with anyone," I grumbled. "Least of all him. We broke up. You know this."

She separated her bread and bacon and egg into a neat pattern and took rotating bites of each. "I think it's super inter-esting that you think there was something to break up. If the two of you were a TV show, you'd be cancelled by now."

Harsh. But not untrue.

"Yeah," I said, waggling my eyebrows at her. "But the fic would be hot."

———

I was heading back to the campsite for our morning rehearsal when I ran into Nightshade himself. I felt him coming before I saw him. His magic is hard to miss — he's like a comet and a thunderstorm all at once. His magic might be ice-based, but my temperature rises when he's nearby, which means that for most of our time together, I'd been running a low grade fever.

Explains a lot about every interaction we've ever had, really.

Today, without Ferd or Viola nearby, he looked — wrong in natural lighting, sort of washed out and grey. I was used to him either glittered and primped for a night out, or rosy and glowing in my bed.

If he was a demon, it wasn't the kind that avoided sunlight, though you'd be hard pressed to find any sunlight today. Jules Nightshade stood under an elegant silver-handled umbrella, watching me approach through the drip and drizzle.

"McClaren," he said evenly. Yeah, no amount of hot and sweaty had got us past the point that we used each other's first names.

"Nightshade. Enjoying the weekend?" That came out bitter, because he wasn't supposed to be here. Even if we were still doing whatever the fuck we'd been doing before, it would have been weird to have him here. Now… it was a trip.

He tilted his head, and I waited for something bitchy to come out. Instead, he took a breath and said. "It's not bad. Miracle Workers are playing later on Stage A, after your show. Want to go see them together?"

I was so taken aback to hear him speaking without being snarky or insulting, it didn't occur to me to say no. Besides, Miracle Workers. I wasn't going to miss that. "Sure," I said after too long a moment. "I, uh. Band practice right now though."

He nodded, said "I'll meet you later," in a clipped voice, and walked away through the drizzle.

I watched him go. And Holly thought Juniper was acting out of character. That was nothing compared to this freak show.

Belatedly I realised, if I was his boyfriend, that would have been a damn appropriate time to ask him what was wrong. But I wasn't, so I didn't. And now we had a … what, date, apparently?

Fuck. We didn't do that. We barely knew how to interact without dance music or our clothes off.

I guess there was gonna be music, at least.

There was no way I was surviving our practice without coffee now.

———

CIRQUE DE CACAO is a favourite haunt back home, and they followed us out here; at least, they had a truck serving mostly chocolate, some coffee drinks, to the thirsty and the unwashed.

I ordered a cappuccino and went around the back of the truck to hold the cup between my hands and warm up before I headed back. There was a slight overhang here, and a waterproofing charm that spread a little further, so I could lean against the side and stay dry.

The coffee smelled good enough to drink, but I hadn't decided yet. Coffee fucks with whatever alchemy connects my drumming to the rest of the band. It keeps the magic quiet but it keeps some important me stuff quiet too, so I leave it as a last resort.

Still, my ex-whatever was acting like he was in a Halloween bodyswap episode of *The Bromancers*, and everyone else was taut as a cello wire, and something was gonna go pop before the end of the day. I didn't want it to be me.

One sip. Just to quiet my head down a little. Maybe a second sip.

"Hey," said a low voice. The cute Goth barista who had made my drink climbed out of the truck holding a keep cup of his own. "Mind if I take my break here? Can't go too far, the other two in there are trainees."

I shrugged. "Your truck, man."

He glanced at my drink, and not so subtly checked me out at the same time. "Aren't you playing later?"

Ohh. I smirked at him, turning up what Holly called 'that ridiculous slutty rock star charisma you hide under dirty t-shirts'. "You're a fan."

Goth Boy looked startled, and a little embarrassed. "Home-town supporter," he corrected. "Makes me sound less needy."

"Yeah, that's definitely working for you." I held out a hand. "Sage."

"Obviously," he said, with a sarcastic quirk of his mouth that I kind of liked. He met my hand with his own and yeah, that was why the coffee tasted so good. His magic was a barely there roll of an ocean wave, subtle and unobtrusive. "Evan."

I took another sip of the coffee, letting the calmness flood through me. I hadn't touched coffee in days, because there wasn't much point if Nightshade and I weren't fucking any more. How messed up was that? "Hey," I said, noticing that Evan wore a How Cinnovar I'll Go t-shirt. "You know that episode with the demon matchmaking? In Season 1?"

A slow smile came over Evan's face. "Sure. That was a good episode. First time we came to canon queer representation in the show."

There was the signal if ever there was one, that it was OK to flirt. *The Bromancers*: providing opportunities for gay nerds to find each other for three years and counting.

But I had a practice to get to.

And...

Nah, there was no and.

"I gotta go," I said, letting myself sound regretful. "See you around, maybe?"

"Hope so," said Evan.

There was a spark when we looked at each other, and one that had nothing at all to do with magical incompatibility. So that was a thing.

I saluted him with my coffee cup and headed back to the campsite before I could admit to myself that I had just performed one of the dorkiest moves in the history of flirting.

———

THE SKY OPENED up as I ran back to the campsite, so I wasn't just being drizzled on any more, but soaked to the skin.

This time it was Viola Vale I met at the mouth of the campsite — like Nightshade, she had her own umbrella, though hers was probably Prada.

Who was I kidding? His was probably Prada too. They like the finer things in life, these Basilisk Brats.

Apart from her stupidly expensive umbrella and her $500 haircut, Viola had done a reasonable job of dressing casual for the festival. Her sneakers were as muddy as everyone else's, and she was wearing a Wingless t-shirt that… damn it, that was another one she'd stolen from me. I didn't even know it had gone missing. She wore it like a dress over leggings, with an actual metal belt slung around her hips to imply that it was made to be worn that way, instead of to stretch over the chest of a normal-sized drummer.

"I liked that shirt," I grumbled.

"You have excellent taste," she said crisply.

Too late, I recognised the fiery expression in her eyes, and the angry tilt of her battle lipstick. Damn it. "What have I done now?"

Viola leaned in, poking me in the gut. "Something's wrong with Jules. You have to fix it with your dick."

"He's not my problem any more," I protested. "And my dick is not actually magic."

I swear her pupils actually flamed on. I could feel the heat of her magic building up — if it hadn't been for those few sips of cappuccino my shirt would have ignited at her touch.

"He's not acting like himself," she snapped. "He's all fake and boring."

"Like a Halloween body swap episode?" I suggested helpfully.

"I don't care about your TV show, Sage. I care about Jules. What's the point of you if you don't make him happy?"

"You'd miss stealing my t-shirts if I was gone."

She rolled her eyes at me. "Sure, whatever helps you sleep at night, you ridiculous cliff face in tight jeans."

When she walked away, she took the rest of my cappuccino with her. I didn't even see her take it from my hand.

―――――

THAT MORNING, we held the worst rehearsal in the history of the band.

I can't even say what was wrong.

Just…

Juniper and Holly were off by the tiniest fraction, both of them giving each other wary looks, and that song was back, beating the sound of its own damned drum inside my skin. There were way too many voices building up in my brain: Vale and Mei and Nightshade and Evan and …

I needed to get completely out of my head.

I needed to set something on fire with my magic.

I needed to get this song down on paper before it clawed its way out of my skull and not in a good way.

I needed to get on my goddamn broom and deal with some ghosts.

After the show.

I could hold it together until after the show.

CHAPTER 11

HOLLY'S RESTING WITCH FACE

SUNDAY

On Sunday, it rained.

Camping is the worst, and camping in the rain? Double worst.

Only that wasn't the worst part.

The worst part was that I was sharing a tent with Juniper, and … I was pretty sure she wasn't Juniper at all.

7 REASONS TO SUPPOSE THAT JUNIPER IS UNDER SOME KIND OF ENCHANTMENT, OR WAS SWAPPED FOR A CHANGELING, OR SOME EQUALLY DIRE SITUATION.

- 1) Juniper made a new friend.
- 2) Juniper stopped paying attention to me.
- 3) Juniper didn't say thank you when I bumped up her solo piece, Stupid Songs About Victorian Novels, to Number 2 in our set list, even though it was a massive compliment.

OK, I realise that those reasons make me sound like a heinous bitch and total crazy person. But I knew Juniper, all right? She wasn't behaving in any of the ways that make sense, for her. And no one else seemed to notice. Hebe and Sage and the rest were wrapped up in their own dramah.

That left me, Queen of the Self-involved, following Juniper around like a lost puppy and analysing every micro-expression to prove I was right.

She and her new bestie dodged me after rehearsal, and I didn't find them for the rest of the day.

- 4) Juniper AVOIDED ME FOR THE REST OF THE DAY. I mean, how many red flags do you need?

Oh and here's a good one:

- 5) Didn't recognise someone who clearly knew her.

Remember Professor Hottie? The foxy older lady with the wicked guitar? Yeah, I'd forgotten her too, it's been a really long weekend.

Anyway, she came to our show tonight, with a couple of others I recognised from that party on the beach. I saw her as we were waiting to go on stage. Juniper was holding Irene in a suspiciously exactly-in-character way, like she knew I was watching her every move.

Then Professor Hottie — Heather — Helena — eh what are the odds I'll need to remember her name — stepped out of the crowd, eyes on me. She smiled.

I went all warm in the pit of my stomach because we came *this* close to making out on the first night of the festival, and she came to our *show*, and I'm super into the attention of attractive older ladies.

Then Professor Hottie saw Juniper, and took on a slightly frostier, less flirtatious expression. Professional, I realised.

Juniper didn't notice. She walked straight past Professor Hottie and on to the stage.

"I'd swear she's in one of my classes," the Professor said thoughtfully to one of her mates.

He laughed and nudged her. "No one expects to see their Professor at something like this."

I remembered Juniper, that first night, all blushing and stammering and "you can't have her, Holly." No way she wouldn't at least give her Professor a polite nod.

I guess, if someone was going to research Juniper Cresswell of Fake Geek Girl, they might not go quite so far as to learn every single person she'd ever met.

It was a crack in the armour. It was a clue. It was totally time to go on stage.

- 6) It's just not her. I know it. I KNOW IT.

Bad rehearsal means great show, except when it doesn't. And yeah, that had been the shittiest practice we'd had through in years. Worse than that time we got food poisoning and I threw up on Sage's drum kit.

Our show today was one of the best sets we'd ever done. There was a fierce, angry electricity running through all of us, and we harnessed it. Sage was on fire, almost literally. Juniper was relaxed, having fun on stage in a way that almost never happens except sometimes late at night when she thinks no one is really paying attention to her.

- 7) Juniper without stage fright, what even is this bullshit?

I sang my fucking heart out.

When we were done, I stormed off stage, grabbed hold of little Ellie Whatsit, Juniper's new BFF, who was standing too close to the steps. I stalked her like a lion, around the back of the stage.

"Hey Holly, great show," she said, trying to shove me off, but my nails were sunk hard into her stupid geeky… hey, I have that exact jacket. Huh.

"What have you done with her?" I snarled into her face. "Where's the real Juniper?"

The fangirl looked innocent for about three seconds, and then she smiled at me, all sugar and spice. "She didn't deserve to be part of the band. She wasn't even having fun."

That spiked my heart. Was it true? Did Juniper want to leave us too? We'd barely recovered from losing Nora.

Then I remembered who I was speaking to. I shook her like a rat. "Give. My. Juniper. Back."

Arms wrapped around me from behind, and Juniper's scent overwhelmed me. Only… that wasn't Juniper's scent at all.

- 8) Juniper doesn't smell like that. She smells like expensive candles and cheap chocolate. What even is that smell…

"Relax," the not-Juniper whispered into my ear, her lips brushing against my earlobe. "It doesn't hurt. And we're going to have so much fun together."

Darkness closed over my head, and took me away.

CHAPTER 12

SAGE HAS NEVER TAKEN A BOY HOME BEFORE, BUT DON'T START THINKING THIS MEANS ANYTHING, OK?

SUNDAY NIGHT

I CAME off that gig sweating and thirsty, fired up like I'd never been before. I almost had the shape of the song now, could feel it beating its way out from the inside of my rib cage.

And I knew where I was gonna find it. Sure I did. Because the song that had been driving me up the wall all week? It kicked off when I first admitted to myself that coming back to Mandrake Sands was gonna stir some shit up.

I needed a broomstick, and I needed a friend.

Holly disappeared straight after the show, and when I saw her again she was flirting with her fans, tossing her hair, high off the performance or maybe some extracurricular potion, who was I to even guess? Juniper was still enjoying her bizarre personality bypass, right at Holly's side. I guess they made up whatever their weird non-fight was about?

Dec and Vale had disappeared somewhere. When did my mates all end up in couples?

Mei hadn't even made it to the show.

Hebe and Ferd at least had the decency to swing by before they went off to get naked together for like, the third time today. They'd been sitting in each other's laps as we played our souls out on stage. Now they came up to pat me on the back and ruffle my hair, getting their hands good and sweaty in the process.

"That was so great," Hebe breathed in my ear.

"Yeah," I said hoarsely. Not much voice left. "You two good?"

"Of course," said Ferd, slinging an arm around Hebe's shoulders.

"Fine," said Hebe, smiling.

My Hebe has the best smile in the known universe. No one can match that smile of hers. This wasn't it.

"Okay, right," I snapped, grabbing her hand, and then his. "C'mon. Let's get this sorted."

The song beating in my head was about to come out of my skull all messy, and I didn't have time to stop and deal with this bullshit, but I could see the future unfolding like a flying carpet crash, with safety charms disabled. I didn't have the time and energy to spend a month watching these two drag their way through the slowest and most painful breakup in history, so...

A couple of tents away from the main stage, it was quieter, so I could hear Ferd and Hebes protesting at me above the sound of the imaginary beat in my head. "Truth bombs. Brace yourselves."

"Sage, you can't just shove your sticky paws into my relationship," Hebe snapped, like she was scared of what I was going to say.

I didn't blame her. I was scared too.

"I don't even," started Ferd, and then stopped.

"Let's make this fast," I blurted out. "Ferd mate, when Hebe and I broke up, she didn't admit she was upset about it for more than six months and when she did, it wasn't to me."

Hebe opened her mouth and then shut it again. "That's fair," she admitted.

Ferd looked like he was just now figuring out something very important.

"Babe," I told her. "I love you, but you're shit at admitting when you're not okay. Just because Holly is a drama queen doesn't mean you have to be a ... couch cushion that everyone sits on, you know?

Hebe glared at me, which was the most fire I'd seen out of her all weekend. "You think I'm a *couch cushion*?"

"Who is the couch in this scenario?" wondered Ferd.

I leaned in and gave him a sweaty smacking kiss on the cheek, then one for Hebe too. "Just — show each other the messy parts, yeah? I'm all for fucking your way through your problems and pretending they're not there, that's totally my brand but you two are way smarter than me. Right?"

And now I was legit giving them advice on their sex life. Time to back the hell off. There was a broomstick calling me. The night wasn't over yet.

"Who died and made you the Boyfriend Police?" Hebe yelled after me, but she was laughing, so maybe I had left them in a better place than I found them. Maybe.

———

I WAS out of options for mates to join me on my Magical Mystery Tour of feelings and tragic backstory, but that was probably how it should be. I talked a good game, but no one wanted to see my messy parts right now.

I considered swinging past that coffee truck, see if the Hot Goth Boy was still serving this late, but how pathetic was that? A light flirting session did not make him my friend. I was on my own.

So yeah I wasn't exactly in the best of moods when I stormed into our campsite to find Jules Fucking Nightshade with his hands all over my broom. "What the hell do you think you're doing to Bruce?"

He jumped, shocked by my presence, and then pulled his usual frosty snark over himself like a cloak. "I'm getting out of here. I didn't want to come in the first place..."

So he hadn't been intending to keep our Miracle Workers date either? I didn't know whether to laugh or be pissed off.

Oh, apparently I was pissed off.

"Hey, it's not my fault you have no free will when your friends are involved," I growled, leaning into his space and snatching my broom directly from his grasp.

His eyes flashed. "Excuse me, are you suggesting *I'm* the one who doesn't set boundaries with his friends? You live with yours like some hippie commune fake family sitcom."

That was… not unfair. "Come on," I said shortly, and shoved Holly's broom at him. Hers was in the best condition because we mostly never let her use it. "You want to fly? Fly with me."

Nightshade arched an eyebrow perfectly, like he was some kind of old school film star. "Where are we going?"

He didn't say no.

Something told me I was gonna regret this, but not yet. Not until morning.

"Trust me," I said.

And what do you know? He did.

———

WE FLEW ABOUT fifteen minutes inland from Mandrake Sands, across some horribly familiar airways. Farming land beneath us, the ground all patchwork like something out of old paintings.

He was good in the air. Of course. When it came to magic, Jules Nightshade is the only person I've ever met who has anything like my raw power. He left frost patterns in the sky as he flew. His proximity made my power spark up, hungry and wanting.

No coffee for either of us in the last several hours. We wouldn't be able to fly these babies if we had.

So this was gonna get explosive.

It was growing dark, the sky curling up at its edges. I found the creek and swooped up the length of it, Nightshade in my tail wind. He overtook me, grinning like this was a drag race.

First genuine 'I'm having fun' smile I'd seen on his face all weekend, though I'd seen a lot of 'I am pretending to have fun because my friends are looking' grimaces.

"Down," I said, and dropped hard, ducking under his flight

path. "We'll wanna be near the ground before we reach that line of trees."

He cupped his ear like he hadn't heard me, but followed as I ran lower and lower.

Half a metre from the tree line, my feet brushed the dusty ground, and I jogged lightly to a standstill, Bruce powering down. Nightshade kept going, circling around, and I saw his mistake a second before it happened.

He wasn't that far up when he fell, only four metres or so, but it was enough to jolt the breath out of him. He threw himself to his feet straight away, like a cat pissed off that you saw it slide off the back of the couch. "What the fuck was that?"

"This is Circe Creek," I said, huffing out a laugh, but not at him.

For a moment, I'd been scared that I got him hurt. Hilarious.

"Hang on, I know that name." Nightshade stared around at the trees and paddocks. "Did you drag me all this way to the Town That Ate Magic?"

"Do they still call it that?"

His gaze raked the tree line, spotting the curse stone where it had been placed nearby, within sight of another, further up the nearest hill. Magic repelling spells, containing the whole small town and surrounding farms for about 400 acres. "So are you planning to murder me, or is this a booty call?"

"Would you believe neither?" I clapped him on the shoulder, more of a bro gesture than we'd ever shared before. "Congrats, Nightshade. I'm taking a tour down memory lane, and you get a front seat ticket to the wallowing and the angst."

He stared at the curse stone. "You grew up here? *Here*?"

I shrugged. "Didn't even know I had magic until my Aunt moved me to the city when I was thirteen."

Nightshade's eyes bugged out. "But you're — you. You have so much magic. Like, a stupid amount."

"Yeah. First wet dream in the new flat, I blew the power in the whole street." He didn't laugh. I guess it wasn't that funny. "Wanna come watch me write something obscene on the town hall?"

Nightshade hugged himself. "If you think I'm setting foot inside this magic-hating, witch-murdering town of yours, you are dumber than most drummers. And that's saying something."

Well, if he put it like that... the appeal of visiting my old haunts melted away. I looked at Nightshade instead, really looked at him. He was pale and drawn, no longer pretending to be the life of the party. I don't think it was just the prospect of sleeping under damp canvas for another night. "So how's your weekend been going?"

"It's been shit, actually," he said distinctly. "Chauv wanted to come here after — but it was a mistake."

"Is Ferd Chauvelin the reason you've been pretending to have a good time?"

His eyes flashed at me. "You didn't think it was for your benefit?"

Well, that was a relief. "So this isn't a stalk and seduce your ex mission?"

Nightshade laughed at that, a short, sharp sound. "Wow, and I thought I'd escaped total humiliation this evening."

"I'm kidding, mate." We weren't mates, not anywhere near it. But maybe we should be. We came from different worlds, but we had a hell of a lot in common when we weren't ripping each other's clothes off. We shared too many friends to ignore each other for the rest of our lives. "What have you got to lose by telling me?"

"It's not my story to tell." He huffed impatiently as I waggled my eyebrows at him. "You're so juvenile, McClaren."

"Didn't stop you wanting to lick my abs." But no, that was... old Sage and Jules. I was trying something else here. "Sorry. Start again."

Both his eyebrows went up this time. "Apologies? We are turning over a new leaf."

"Nightshade," I growled.

He relented. "Chauv's family are... I mean, I never thought of them as warm. Warmer than my parents, but that's not saying much: my Maman was carved out of a sarcasm iceberg. But his family? They treat him like..." He trailed off, lost for words.

I grunted in sympathy, and waved a hand at the curse markers. "Like this town treats witches?"

"*Yes*. Like they might catch something from him, what the fuck? He lost his magic in a freak lab accident, it's not like he married a stripper or groped the maid or whatever."

I blinked. "There is so much wrong with that sentence."

Nightshade was in full flight now. "We didn't even make it to brunch," he ranted. "Got a head's up from one of his cousins that we were walking into an intervention, not a reunion. I guess the parents had been all scheming together. They weren't up to date with Vale and I — you know."

Yeah. Nightshade and Vale froze Ferd out after the accident that took his magic — or he froze them out. He'd changed his university allegiances, made new friends, found Hebe. It was only in the last few months that he reconnected with his old friends, and we ended up all tangled up in each other. Now, you needed a chalk diagram or advanced software to unravel the complex dating-and-fucking connections between Ferd's two social groups.

"They thought we'd help them screw him over," Jules said bitterly. "That we'd encourage him to sign on the dotted line for surgical intervention, all for the incredibly slim possibility he can return to his old life without them having to change the way they think about anything, you know? So we bailed. I was hoping we could spend the weekend clubbing or binge-eating to get his mind off it but oh no, Chauv and Vale insisted we come here, to hang with their sweeties." He glared at me. "You and me, we're done. I'm not trying to stealth reverse the breakup or whatever."

"What makes this different to all the other times we broke up and jumped back into bed again a few weeks later?" I had to ask, because I genuinely wanted to know. "What changed?"

Nightshade gave me the frostiest of glares. "Believe it or not, I decided I want a boyfriend who actually likes me."

Ha, wow. A whole night of truth bombs.

"It's fine," I shrugged, shoving down the small stab of completely deserveable hurt. "Believe it or not, I don't spend my days thinking about you and me and the grand romance we might have had."

"Join the club," he said, with a sour note that made me take a second look.

Jules Nightshade looked *wrecked*. The good news was, I wasn't the reason for it. But now I was paying attention to something other than how good his mouth tasted on mine... well, some pieces clicked into place.

Ferd Chauvelin was a good bloke. He could be a wanker at times when the silver-dipped wand started to show, but he'd made an effort to break the worst of his rich boy programming. He treated Hebe with respect, and he was on my All-time Flatmates Who Don't Suck list. (I booted Dec off that list months ago when I found clay in the fridge for the fourteenth time)

I liked Ferd. But the bloke could be super oblivious. He hadn't even noticed his girlfriend was fighting with him.

He hadn't noticed that Jules was miserable about being here.

Speaking of oblivious. How much of an idiot was I for not spotting before now that Jules Nightshade, shallow, hyper-privileged magical genius arsehole extraordinaire, was completely fucked up over his straight best friend?

"That must suck," I said aloud.

Jules looked at me, annoyed. "What?"

"Nothing, mate." Damn it. I'd been so sure I needed to shove Jules out of my life. But now? The poor bastard clearly needed more than two friends. "I think this is the first real conversation we've ever had," I observed.

He leaned against a tree, recovering some of his usual poise. "Yes, you should take me to scary isolated murder sites more often."

"I don't think anyone's been murdered in this town since the summer before I left," I said, and waggled my eyebrows at him.

He snorted. "I will pay you not to tell me that story."

After a minute, I realised he was staring at me expectantly. "What?"

Jules waved a hand. "Aren't you planning to, I don't know. Wallow in nostalgia while you walk up and down the tiny three-horse town that deprived you of magic for the first thirteen years of your life? Isn't that why we're here?"

Well, that was the original plan. "Changed my mind," I said aloud. "I'm gonna not, and say I did. Let's go find a pub and get blitzed."

Jules Nightshade smiled slowly. "I guess you are the smartest drummer that I know."

I was gonna friend the hell out of this bloke. He wouldn't know what hit him.

CHAPTER 13
HEBE & THE FANGIRLS

MONDAY, EARLY HOURS

So IT WAS EMBARRASSING that Ferd and I had been called on our bullshit by my ex, but it worked.

I was going to be able to tease Sage until the end of time for being invested enough to interfere in our relationship. Really, it was more embarrassing for him.

We talked. We really talked.

Ferd told me how his friends had saved him from yet another horrible intervention with his family. He'd had something of a breakdown in front of Jules and Viola, which he was embarrassed about. He'd been keeping up a front with them before now, pretending he didn't really mind how his parents were treating him.

"Even if I had my magic back," he said softly. "I don't think I could go back to them, to the family, that life. Not now I know how little they value me."

I kind of yelled at him a bit, because come on. I wouldn't have been mad if I'd known why he wanted to be here. If I'd known he needed me. I wasted most of the weekend being pissed off over small stuff because he was hiding the big stuff.

Huh. Sage McClaren, drummer and relationship guru. Hilarious, considering he hasn't had a steady someone in years.

That was a thought for another time, because Ferd and I had a lot of making up to do.

We walked on the beach for a while, and talked, and then we went back to his brand new shiny tent for more talking and touching and… well, sex is a lot more fun when you're not using it to avoid difficult conversations.

Before we slept, I summoned all the sound-muffling hex bags into a circle around the tent, just in case we wanted to do it all over again in the morning.

That was the reason I didn't realise what else was happening in our campsite until it was far too late.

———

I WOKE up naked and warm inside a sleeping bag built for two, with my boyfriend's firm arms crowding me into the air mattress. There are worse ways to wake up.

For the first time since I set up the campsite, my magic was calm and quenched, completely content. Back in its box until the next time it reared its domestic goddess/monster tendrils.

Except.

There was an itch.

Just a tiny sting, like an ant or a beetle. A pin-prick of alertness.

It was quiet out there. Sound-muffling hex bags work both ways.

Ferd sighed and muttered against me, sliding his face down to his favourite place, between my breasts. Utterly unhelpful. I unzipped the sleeping bag and slipped out, tucking a pillow in with him so that he wouldn't wake up.

His tent, so his clothes. I pulled on my jeans from yesterday and took a singlet and flowing blue silk shirt (seriously, silk for camping?) out of his rucksack and pulled those on. I borrowed clean socks, to wear under my boots (this is Australia, you never set foot in a campsite with bare feet). Ferd is a seemingly endless supplier of clean socks; he always has several pairs handy. It's one of the things that my magic most enjoys about him.

I unzipped the tent and stepped out into chaos.

———————

IT WAS some kind of party — noisy and raucous. Perhaps 40 people crammed into our campsite, dancing and laughing and drinking.

I checked my watch. It was 3am.

My magic rose up in me, unsure whether it wanted to welcome the guests with cocktails and snacks, or fling them all out. I looked around for a familiar face, trying to figure out which of my friends had invited this lot.

My sister rose up out of the mob, covered in glitter and smugness. Well, sure. This wasn't the first time Holly had sprung an unexpected party on my living space, though she was usually sensible enough to invite everyone to the boys' flat instead of ours.

She was wearing a t-shirt with her own face on it, which was… odd. Holly adores the Fake Geek Girl merch but she's too cool to wear it in public.

Everyone was wearing Fake Geek Girl gear. It crept up on me quickly, that realisation. Some of it was official merch, some was homemade. Lots of *Bromancers* shirts and *Athena Owl* snuggies. There were at least four men wearing some kind of Sage cosplay, which was a special kind of surreal.

Juniper was dancing with one of the fake drummers, her arms wrapped around his not-wide-enough shoulders.

Holly saw me, and her face lit up. "Favourite sister!" she demanded, and gave me the world's biggest hug.

My magic wanted to smother her with a pillow.

"We should sing together, sweetie," she muttered with her face mashed into my cheek.

"We should — what?" Was she high? This had better not be Troll again, she was the worst on drugs. Never like this, though. I shoved her away from me. "What exactly —"

"You are the cutest," Holly giggled, and booped my nose. "Come on, let's sing Big Gay Breakup Song together. Juniper can film it for the website. It'll be *amaze*."

And then I knew what my magic had been trying to tell me. I stared at her, cold from my feet to my fingertips. "You're not my sister."

She hesitated only for a fraction of a second. "C'mon Hebes, don't be a drag…"

I reached out for her, my magic welling up in me like I was going to explode, like I was Sage-as-a-teenager, all power and no control. Like I was going to burn the world. "WHAT HAVE YOU DONE WITH MY SISTER?"

She wasn't Holly. But she sure as hell looked afraid of me. "I don't…"

"Get out," I said, very calmly, and not to her.

Domestic magic, even the gentle and embarrassingly gender-essentialist kind, has many uses. Mine had gone through such an emotional workout this weekend, it was on a hair trigger.

One of the first defensive spells the Mums ever taught me was the Eviction Enchantment. It only take two air runes and a few firm words, if your magical affinity is bound in house and home.

The campsite was mine, no matter what stamp Jules Nightshade and the others had put on it. I formed the runes with my fingers, and said the words.

The party vanished. I heard the muffled cries and protests as every unwanted visitor found themselves unexpectedly mashed in a pile, just outside on the path.

Holly — not Holly, as it turned out — was still in front of me. Juniper — *not Juniper*, Holly had been so sure of it and I hadn't listened — was here too, looking wide-eyed and guilty, nervous in a completely different way to Juniper's legit nervous face.

I'd been so wrapped up in my own stupid feelings, I had missed something really awful happening right under my nose.

"What did you do?" I demanded.

Not-Holly gave a weak laugh. "It's just for fun," she started to say.

I snapped.

My magic snapped.

There was a blinding haze that smelled of violets and cinnamon, and the earth literally quaked beneath us, rippling for a moment. When I could see straight again, there was a floral grandma couch where the campfire used to be, and both girls sat on it, pinned tightly by homicidal lace throw covers.

"WHERE IS MY SISTER?" I yelled at them. "WHERE IS MY FRIEND?"

Tents started unzipping. Sound muffling charms — and there must have been more than mine at work here — didn't stop you feeling vibrations of the earth. Viola and Dec stumbled out, half-dressed, ready for a fight. Mei emerged, a mirror in each hand. Finally Ferd, wearing nothing but a pair of hastily-pulled-on jeans.

I heard cursing and shoving, and Sage and Jules appeared up the path, rumpled and sweaty, each holding a broom.

"What the fuck is with the fan convention out the front?" Sage demanded, making a beeline for me. "Babe, I felt you from a kilometre away, what's going on?"

Ferd flicked him an irritated look at the 'babe,' but came to my side too. "Hebe?"

I pointed at the two girls on the sofa. "Halloween body swap episode," I managed to choke out, infusing it with all the anger running through my body. Not a joke. So not a joke.

"Aw, *hell*," said Dec.

Sage, Jules and Viola, the three most powerful witches in our friends group, turned upon the imposters, eyes flashing with magic.

"Where are your real bodies?" snarled Sage.

The fake Holly lifted her chin defiantly, but Jules created a glowing iceball in his left fist. A smell like an electrical storm began to roll off Sage.

"I'd answer the question," said Viola crisply. Smoke was actually beginning to pour out of the cuffs of her elegant designer pyjamas. "We can find them without your help. But you'll want all the brownie points you can earn if you expect us to show mercy at some point in the future."

Not Juniper muttered the map references for their camp.

"We'll go," Jules told Sage, then motioned to Viola and Ferd. Ferd hesitated, and brushed my cheek with a light kiss before he went with his friends, knowing of course that Sage wouldn't want to leave my side.

I loved him so much.

I should tell him more often.

———

SAGE and I rarely work magic together. Our styles aren't exactly compatible. But when Ferd and the others brought the two unconscious fangirls into our camp, along with the book detailing the spell they had used to possess Holly and Juniper, and several representatives from Winterfest Security, well...

It had to be both of us. His spark, and my hearth.

It was mostly another version of the Eviction Enchantment. With Sage's power bleeding into mine, there was a smoothness to it, an ease I'd never felt before, even when it came to the simplest forms of my magic: feeding people, keeping them safe and clean.

There's no one else Sage would trust enough to hand over the keys to everything he was capable of doing. He had the juice, but I had the control. Holding things in is my relationship flaw, but it's also my superpower. We had to do this right, and carefully. We couldn't afford to leave any damage.

Holly and Juniper opened their eyes, and the right people looked back at us.

"I'm going to kill them," was the first thing Holly said.

Juniper burst into tears.

Holly turned around and flung her arms around Juniper protectively. "Sage can kill them," she said benevolently.

"Too many witnesses," said Sage.

"We'll take your statements now," said the Head of Winterfest Security with a discreet cough. "The police are on their way."

"Okay," I said shakily. "Okay."

Viola Vale, standing nearest to me, gave me a worried look as if she thought I might hug her. She pushed Ferd at me instead.

Ferd gave the best hugs. "I want to go home," I told his left shoulder as he wrapped me up like a parcel in his arms.

"If we pack up and leave before breakfast," said Mei in an undertone. "We could be home by the time *The Bromancers* drops."

I leaned around Ferd's hug to glare at her across the campsite.

"Which… is not actually important right now," she added. "Obviously."

"No, it is," Ferd said fiercely, hugging me harder. "Let's go home, all of us, and you can watch your show."

Oh yes. I loved him.

CHAPTER 14

THE INTIMATE THOUGHTS OF MISS JUNIPER CRESSWELL, CELLIST AND COMMITTED BROMANCERS FANGIRL.

MONDAY

DEAR DIARY

The part I'm having the hardest time reconciling myself to is that those girls were our fans. Our audience. They loved us. They wanted to be us, for a while.

It wasn't a joke or a prank. They actually wanted to take our places in the world. Like they could do a better jobs of living our lives.

I could understand if they wanted to be beautiful, talented, charming Holly. I could understand if they wanted to be the powerful magical genius with drum-kit that is Sage.

The part I couldn't quite wrap my head around was the girl who wanted to be *me*. I barely want to be me, most days. I'm nothing special. I've never quite been pretty enough, or thin enough, or confident enough. My family thinks I'm wasting my musical talent. My friends…

As it turns out, my friends are pretty great. And I have more of them than I imagined. Viola Vale spent most of her trip home working on a protection amulet which she later bound around my wrist, saying "Chauvelin would be furious if we let this happen to you again, Cresswell. So don't take it off. Ever."

I didn't even think she knew my name.

After we gave our statements to the police, Sage drove the van back from Mandrake Sands. Holly and Hebe took the car, because Hebe wasn't willing to let Holly out of her sight, and I rode in the back because Holly wasn't willing to let me out of her sight. No one argued about it.

Dec, without anyone else prompting him, confiscated all of Mei's devices, including mirrors and communication charms as well as her phone and laptop, so she wouldn't be spoiled for the *Bromancers* finale. We left Mandrake Sands two hours later than we had hoped — it would air before we got home.

The flying carpet crew arrived back at the Manic Pixie Dream House first, and collected all doonas, blankets, cushions and beanbags from both flats, piling them on the floor in the downstairs living room. It was somewhere between a nest and a pillow fort by the time Mei's little VW pulled up, closely followed by the van.

Hebe kissed Ferd soundly for his work, causing Jules and Viola to complain they weren't getting any of the credit, though of course neither of them especially wanted her to start kissing them.

Holly, still alarmingly possessive, snagged an arm around my waist, insisting I share a beanbag with her as we watched.

I…

I know better to think it means anything. She's still Holly, and I'm still me. I'm not getting my hopes up in any romantic direction. I'm not stupid.

But it means the world to me, that she's the one who noticed I was gone. That she missed me. That she fought for me. That right now, she doesn't want to be anywhere but here, resting her chin on my shoulder, watching an episode of a show she doesn't care about, with our friends.

She's my friend, and I love that.

It's enough.

————

THE CLOSING CREDITS RAN, and our group was silent for a moment.

MEI:

Holy &*^#!@$#$%^%^* (*swear words deleted*)

SAGE:

(*very long sentence made up mostly of swearing*)

HEBE (*punching Ferd in the arm*):

Cinnovate is canon, Cinnovate is canon!

HOLLY:

Which one is Cinnovate?

VIOLA:

Was he the pretty one?

FERD:

Tate's the werewolf bro, Cinnovar is the mysterious seer who lurks in shadows and talks about doom all the time.

JULES:

Eli's the bro who's not a werewolf and wasn't kissing anyone, but took his shirt off three times in the opening credits.

VIOLA:

You've both been secretly watching this show without me.

FERD:

I pay attention to my girlfriend's interests, don't know what Nightshade's excuse is.

JULES:

He took his *shirt* off three *times* in the opening *credits*.

MEI:

Where are my devices? Where's my mirror?
I don't know what to think!

DEC:

Breathe, Mei. You'll figure it out.

MEI:

But but but.

DEC:

I know, right?

MEI (*hint of sadness*):
But it wasn't the *bros*.

SAGE:

Mei. Babe. You've been a Cinnovate shipper forever.

MEI:

But bros…

SAGE:

OK it would have been groundbreaking TV
if Eli & Tate had hooked up. But… Cinnovar and Tate, that's
also pretty ^%@#$ awesome, right?

DEC:

Yeah, c'mon Mei. One of the highest paid actors in US TV just
kissed one of the other highest paid actors in US TV on the
mouth. And you got to watch it in HD and comfort. You've had
worse days.

MEI:

OMG I have to talk to the Internet right now.

And the MirrorWeb. Simultaneously.

SAGE:
Don't get keyboard-burn on your fingertips again.

(*MEI disappears from the scene in a cloud of squee*)

HEBE (*knocking foreheads with Sage*):
So what did you think of the episode?

SAGE:
I think Cinnovar's gonna break Tate's heart.
No way this doesn't end up with misery and
dead bisexuals all over Season 4.

HEBE:
So what, you think they should have got
Eli and Tate together instead?

SAGE (*with covert look at Jules Nightshade
that he thinks no one noticed*):
Nah. It's pretty cool that the bros are
gonna stick to being friends.
As long as *someone's* getting laid in this show.
Gentlewitches and ladygerms,
shall we lay bets now on how many
times shirts come off next season?

MEI (*from the kitchen*):
All the shirts!

HOLLY (*leaning very close to me*):
Are shirts optional in this show a lot?

MISS JUNIPER:
Every other week. But it doesn't really
make sense if you start from here, the first

two episodes explain so much…

HOLLY (*big sigh*):
Fine. Let's start from the beginning.

MISS JUNIPER:
You want to watch *The Bromancers* with us?
Like, all of it, from the beginning?

HOLLY:
Sure. Just with you, though.
Don't tell my sister I'm interested.
She'll be too smug.

MISS JUNIPER:
I guess we can watch them in my room over at halls?

HOLLY:
I'm all yours.

MISS JUNIPER:
(*lost for words*)

MISS JUNIPER:
(*out of words error*)

MISS JUNIPER:
Sounds great. Okay. Um. Let's do that, then.

(*Kermit flail*)
(*Kermit flail*)
(*Kermit flail*)

CHAPTER 15
SAGE AND THE BRO'D TRIP

MONDAY ARVO

THERE'S ONLY SO MUCH FOUND family togetherness I can take.

I love my mates, and my band, and hell even Ferd's weirdo posh hangers on, they're all right.

But Cinnovate kiss or no Cinnovate kiss, I was in no place to be around other people.

As the nesting and viewing party started to morph into an actual party, with mirrors used to project kissing gifs all over the walls, I slipped out without anyone noticing I was gone.

I went downstairs to Dec's art studio garage and wrote my song out, all over a pad of paper from the stash he kept in a drawer for me, when I was driving him up the wall. You know someone's a true blue mate when he makes a special trip to Officeworks on your behalf.

The paper has little drums printed on it. The pens are purple with glitter. Sweet.

It wasn't good yet, the song, but it was something. It was raw and real and mine. More importantly, it was written. Finally. On the fucking page.

Holly found me, an hour or two later. She had changed into pyjamas, though it was the middle of the day on a Monday. Students, right? We're animals.

She also had two stubbies fresh out of the fridge, and who was I to turn down a friendly beer?

"Come on, then," Holly said, swallowing from her own bottle. "Song me."

I passed the pad over and she read critically, underlining a few words and phrases. "Bloody hell, Sage," she said when she was done. "Is that what you've had in your head all week? No wonder you were driving everyone up the wall."

"Don't be jealous, babe, I know that's usually your job…"

"Piss off," she laughed, and read the song again. "This is… I mean, it's not there yet. But it could be really good. All this stuff about — living without magic, living with too much magic. The shit they put you through when you were a kid. The double meaning in the 'baby, where have you been all my life' refrain. It's — this could be huge. Like, mainstream huge. This is your ballad, Sage."

"It's not really Fake Geek Girl though, is it?"

She raised her eyebrows at me. "Looking to go solo, sweetie?" Which yeah, I was aware of the irony. Biggest fight we had this year was when I thought Holly was looking to build a career away from us, ditching Fake Geek Girl for the mainstream.

"I figured I'd sell it," I huffed. "That agent who sold the song I wrote for Kraken, the one that got on the radio? He's been asking for more stuff. Could make some serious bucks."

Holly's eyes went chilly, unimpressed. "Sure. Fine. Of course you could."

"But?" Suddenly I wanted nothing in the world so much as her opinion. Holly is the most selfish, brilliant person I know. She's crazed, but there's a light in her. Music for her is like magic for me. It fills her up, sets her on fire.

Hebe would tell me to do what was best for myself, and Dec would say a whole lot of not much, with some calculated silences left so I could figure out the right choice on my own. But Holly?

Holly would pick the band over me, every time. I needed that.

"I want this," she said now, fingernails digging into the

paper. "I don't want you to sell it to Kraken or some other band who will turn it into a big hit. I want to sing it. I want you to sing it. There's a part for cello in here, I know there is."

"Yeah," I admitted, letting out the truth with a big breath. "There really is."

"I don't care if it's not about geeky shit, I don't care if it's off brand," she said fiercely. "We get this one, Sage. We can do it. Yeah?"

I'd never wanted to hug her so much in my life. "Yeah."

She waved the song at me. "Did you really go back to that craphole town this weekend?"

"Nah," I laughed. "Meant to, but I got sidetracked with Nightshade. Never made it past the curse markers."

"We should go," she said. "Get in the van and just — road trip to Circe Creek. You and me. Work on the song on the way, and paint that stupid magic-hating town all the shades of the super gay rainbow. Hmm," she added with a frown. "Maybe not just us. We should bring Juniper. I think she's been feeling left out of the loop."

"You and me in a van, though," I said skeptically.

An unfamiliar expression crossed Holly's face. Lack of confidence? It didn't suit her. "I know you'd rather hang out with Hebe. But she's all boyfriended up, and…"

"No," I said quietly. "Hol, you know — you're important to me too, right?"

Hebe's been my best friend for years, before and after she was my one true girlfriend. But Holly is mine too. That moment in the campsite when I realised she was gone and I hadn't even… that moment, before the anger hit, that was the most scared I'd ever been in my life.

She stared at me now, seeing the authentic truth in my eyes. "Well, this is embarrassing. For you."

I groaned. "Babe."

"I hate to break it to you, bro, but our love can never be."

"Holly, c'mon."

"You're an out and proud homosexual, and I could never love a drummer. I mean, I have some standards."

"I hate you so much right now."

She hugged me so fast it was somewhere between an embrace and a slap on the butt. "I love you too, you giant bag of dicks. Let's celebrate our true bromance with a platonic road trip to the town that tried to squash all the magic out of you. We'll take your song apart and put it back together until it's so amaze, even our judgiest, geekiest fans will fall in love with it."

Yeah. I wanted that.

"Let's do it," I agreed.

"Awesomesauce." She was making one of her lists already, stealing from my paper and purple glitter pen stash. "So we're gonna hex cock-and-balls graffiti to the walls of your old school…Leave Fake Geek Girl flyers in the public loos? Maybe walk up and down the Main Street a few times looking like punk rock hooligans, see if someone asks us to leave town. Am I gonna need a cowboy hat? I think I'm gonna need a cowboy hat. Possibly a duelling sword. And my sluttiest top, obviously."

We fought all the time, like cats and dogs and bats and owls. Like siblings. When rehearsals got rough, we tore each other to pieces. Sometimes I forgot how well Holly got me.

"All those things," I promised her. "Also we can visit the pub, where I guarantee an awkward silence will fall the second we step inside."

Holly unironically clapped her hands. "Best plan ever."

"Fine," I agreed. "Pack a bag of trashy outfits, write a note for Hebe, grab Juniper. Let's go."

Fake Geek Girl were hitting the road, all over again. We were gonna make magic together — magic, music and a whole lot of trouble.

"It still needs a title," I said suddenly. "My song."

"Don't worry about it," said Holly with a shrug. "We'll think one up on the way. A really good one — good enough to name the album after."

Sneaky wench. "Excuse me, but our next album already has a kickarse title."

She rolled her eyes at me. "We're not calling our next album *Resting Witch Face*, Sage."

Sure we weren't.

"It's a long road ahead of us," I told her. "Plenty of time to change your mind."

"Yeah," said Holly. "Good luck with that, *babe*."

It was like the whole road trip unrolled before us, letting us know exactly what we were gonna fight about over the next few days.

I couldn't wait.

THE ALCHEMY OF FINE

OR: HOW THE BAND GOT TOGETHER, A VERY FAKE GEEK GIRL PREQUEL

THIS STORY BEGINS 15 MONTHS BEFORE FERD MEETS HEBE, AND RUNS BACKWARDS FROM THERE. YES, ON PURPOSE. I REGRET NOTHING.

CHAPTER 1

HOLLY & HEBE & SAGE & NORA & JUNIPER ARE ALL PRETTY DAMN FINE

FINE IS a positive word when applied to the weather. It doesn't mean 'barely making it over the line' like it does when it's applied to feelings, or anything messy like that.

Fine means sunny and bright. A good day.

Today is a good day. The weather's fine.

Holly and her crew totes rejected the Belladonna University End of Year Summer Solstice Picnic when they first heard about it. It sounded like a whole bunch of fake school spirit and unnecessary sunshine.

But.

They have nothing better to do. So here they are.

Sun garlands and glittering tinsel are scattered all around the campus, except for the bare patches where decorations have been stolen by cheeky students looking to adorn themselves, their broomsticks and their residential halls.

Somewhere, snags are sizzling on a grill. Somewhere else, cold tinnies are being sold out of giant tubs of melted ice, to raise money for some vital cause. Cheap beer is fine if it's for a) students and b) charity.

All around Holly, the Real and Unreal students of Belladonna U are drinking, eating, making out, getting sunburnt and listening to terrible music.

It's a good day. The weather's fine.

Sage and Nora, pissed off about having to postpone their 'elves rolling dice with tiny dolls and way too much reading' game for such a mainstream social gathering, have buried themselves in a tote bag full of comics, and a picnic basket of weirdly healthy snacks.

Holly is gonna get a snag in white bread with sauce, as soon as she can be bothered moving from this super comfy tree trunk she is leaning against. No lentil chips for her.

Here's to surviving their first year of uni.

No, they *rocked* their first year of uni.

Holly Hallow now has a queer girl rock band, with Sage as the token gay bloke on the grounds that he's an excellent drummer, and no other band is allowed to steal him. She has friends. She goes to class sometimes. She's had a couple of terrible boyfriends, a fling with a glamorous international student called Monique, and crushes on two of her professors. She has a share house she loves, with family and friends tucked in close around her.

(She cooked for said friends exactly once, producing a series of Instagram-perfect molecular gastronomy salads and decorative pavlova crumbs which caused great outcry and protest among her flatmates because apparently she doesn't understand the definition of comfort food. No one asked her to contribute to their shared Saturday lunch ritual a second time which is just how she likes it)

Only this week, Fake Geek Girl — their awesome band, she's so proud — recorded a second song to put up on YouTube, after the first one did stupidly well. They haven't hit Publish yet. Maybe later today.

Holly has a new song she's itching to write, but it's not quite cooked. Something about loving people who love stupid geeky shit, and how awesome she is for tolerating their deviant behaviour.

"Can you believe it's been a year, Hebes?" Sage sprawls out on the grass, a rare moment of lazy relaxation for him. You wouldn't guess that he hates the outdoors.

Nora, all in black with her eyes hidden behind reflective

sunglasses, lies with her head on Sage's leg, reading an X-Men comic and ignoring them all.

Hebe, Holly's favourite twin sister in all the world, is on the other side of Sage, head resting on the slight padding of his stomach. She's reading something on her phone, holding it as far from Sage as possible so that his ridic all-powerful magic doesn't spark against the tech.

Sage, the phone killer, destroyer of technology. Sage, who charged through all kinds of advanced extension courses as a first year student, because his professors have picked up on how goddamned powerful he is. Sage, certified goofball and A-grade dork who somehow finds time to hit the gym four times a week.

Keeping him was a good call, Holly concedes from her comfy spot, pressed between a sturdy tree trunk and the equally sturdy Juniper, who might or might not be asleep on Holly's shoulder. Sage adds value.

"A year what?" mumbles Hebe, not really paying attention.

"A year since, you know." Sage shrugs awkwardly without dislodging either of the women using his personal wall of beef-steak as furniture. He hums a bar of what is now officially titled Big Gay Breakup Song. Holly considers it her masterwork.

"Since we…?" says Hebe.

"Uh, yes."

"Oh."

Holly holds her breath, but only for a couple of seconds before her sister laughs. Hebe lifts her head slightly and thunks it back down against the soft part of Sage's stomach so he goes 'oof.' "You mean, since you rom com ran your way to my doorstep to break up with me?" she says lightly, eyes back on her phone. "Good times."

It's a *great* day. The weather's fine.

Holly breathes, smiling to herself as Sage and Hebe bicker, the two of them finally comfortable with themselves in a way they haven't been all year, not really, though they've both been pretending really hard.

The mood shifts when Hebe mentions some boy she agreed

to go out with later. Sage, on dangerously thin ice, doesn't reckon the bloke is good enough for her.

Sage, whose taste in men is so bad it makes Holly's own boyfriends look like beautiful, emotionally well-adjusted rocket scientists in comparison.

Hebe raises both her eyebrows, and Holly braces herself for whatever terrible, sharp and wounded words might come out of her sister's mouth. "At least…" says Hebe, "…Kyle isn't under the impression that I am my own twin sister."

Sage groans with his entire body. "Are you ever going to let that one drop?"

"Not while the world is turning," Hebe grins, completely relaxed about teasing him.

Oh, Holly thinks in relief. *So that's what fine looks like. It suits her*.

"I haven't heard this story," chimes in Nora.

"Hang on," says Holly, catching up. "*I* haven't heard this story. Sage, you galah. Did you still think Hebes was me when you first asked her out? Fifteen-year-old you was a disaster."

Hebe laughs, her head jiggling against Sage's stomach. "He figured out one of us was the music twin and one of us was the geeky twin but he mixed up our names."

"Wow," says Holly, wincing. "Near miss, McClaren."

"You're telling me," Sage snarks. "I like to think my fifteen-year-old subconscious knew better than I did."

"Well," says Holly, deadpan. "I wouldn't say it was 100% on the right track."

Sage gives her a startled look, all *you went there*, and Holly offers a smug look in return.

Hebe snorts.

"How did you know it was going to work?" Juniper murmurs, pressing a little closer to Holly. Awake after all. "The band, I mean. All the parts coming together. We're all so different."

Sage opens his mouth, and Holly can tell he's about to launch his 'musical collaboration is alchemy' speech. "It's not *magic*," she breaks in, interrupting him before he can say a word. "It's just people. Any combination of people can mix, as long as they, you know. Bend a bit."

"I didn't know flexibility was your strong suit," says Hebe.

Holly sniffs. "I don't have to bend. Everyone else can bend around me."

"So not magic, just bullying," says Sage. "Sounds about right."

"Ice cream!" says Nora, jumping up. "That dodgy ice cream van just restocked. Who wants one?"

"I'll help." Sage rolls Hebe carefully off his stomach before climbing to his feet and cracking his back. "Any chance we can eat them somewhere with walls and a roof?"

"Grass isn't going to kill you," Nora mocks him.

Juniper wanders after them. Holly watches her go. Somehow Juniper has retained all her softness through a year surrounded by hard-edged cynics. It's admirable.

"So," says Hebe after a few minutes, one hand shading her eyes from the bright sun. "First year at Belladonna U worked out fine, don't you think, Hol?"

There's that word again. "*Fine* is boring," Holly pronounces. "I want next year to be half terrible and half amazeballs. Like, a car crash of awesome with a side salad of WTF."

"Yes," says Hebe patiently. "But that's because you're a very dramatic person."

"I am not dramatic!" flounces Holly. "You take that back or I'll destroy everything that you love."

"What are we talking about?" asks Sage, returning with Nora, Juniper and handfuls of ice creams. "I heard death threats, must be good."

"Next year," says Holly. "Which is going to be unforgettable. I think we should each do something crazy outside our comfort level."

Hebe blinks. "Hol, do you have a comfort level? What would outside of it even look like?"

"I'll find something. Juniper!" says Holly quickly.

Juniper startles, as she often does when Holly addresses her directly. "Um, what? Okay."

Holly points a finger at her. "You are going to write a song for the band. Your own song."

Juniper looks intrigued and horrified. "Right. Yes. If you think I can…"

"Sage. You are going to admit to your course advisor that you actually are planning to do a triple major." Holly glares at him. "Doing one by stealth is not practical. Honesty saves time."

"I hate you but you're probably right," admits Sage.

"Hebe," says Holly, pointing her finger of power. "You will come out raging with me one night a month. No complaints, no protests, no attempts to write essays in nightclubs."

"Fine," says Hebe, obviously aware she is getting off lightly. "What are you going to —"

"Nora," says Holly.

Nora holds up her hand. "I'm a year ahead of you lot. Next year, I am completing all my classes. That's it. Band practice and studying. I like my comfort zone just fine."

Nora will be graduating before the rest of them. That's… a problem to deal with next year, not now.

"You will wear a colour other than black every day for a week," Holly says finally, filing that other and far more uncomfortable thought to the back of her head.

Nora frowns. "Fine. But I get to pick your thing."

"Okay…" Holly agrees warily. Better than Sage or Hebe picking for her, right? Right?

Nora grins with all her teeth. "You are going to participate in a full D&D campaign. Tabletop. Miniatures. The works."

Holly's mouth falls open in horror. "No. With the plastic wizards in unreasonably long robes? NO."

Sage and Hebe are hooting with delight.

"You can borrow my dice!" squeals Hebe.

"I will totally help you design your character," says Sage. "How do you feel about goblins?"

"No, she could totally pull off dragon healer," Hebe argues. The two of them fall into a conversation in which the word 'orc' is mentioned far too often. Hebe consults a 'character sheet app' on her phone. The world is ending.

Holly stares at them both. They're finishing each other's sentences, they're so excited. This is high school all over again — the good parts of high school, Hebe and Sage so in sync with each other. They really are going to stay friends.

Holly probably doesn't need the band any more, to keep Sage from falling out of their lives.

Juniper smiles shyly at Holly, and moves a little closer. "Do you think you could help me? Write my song. I've never actually done that before, the words part. I can do melody…"

"Make a list of shit you love," advises Nora. "Or shit that drives you nuts. That's the best place to start. Holly is the best person to help with the technical parts. She's got like, a natural talent for composition, it's super annoying."

Yeah, Holly doesn't need the band any more.

But.

She's gonna keep it anyway.

CHAPTER 2

THE MANIC PIXIE DREAM HOUSE IS A TOWER OF COMFORT

COMFORT LUNCH WAS Dec's idea. Dec is Hebe's favourite of Sage's roommates because he's a geek, which she understands, and he isn't a dick about Real studies being somehow more important than Unreal, like Matteus who actually sneered when he found out she and Juniper were studying Literature and Gender Studies.

It's a random Saturday halfway through their second semester of first year at Belladonna U. The band played a party last night, and they're still riding on the high of an appreciative audience. They played mostly covers but some of their own songs, and no one hated them.

Turns out, not being hated is Fake Geek Girl #goals. Hebe would never have guessed.

A most amazing smell comes wafting down the stairs from the flat above: garlic and butter and spices.

"Lunch!" Dec yells down the stairs. "Come and get it!"

Sage refers to their place as the Manic Pixie Dream House, claiming they are the vanguard of some kind of post-apocalyptic arts-and-geekery commune. He and Dec like to pretend they are in a niche reality TV show for gaming nerds, which drives no-sense-of-humour Matteus up the wall. He is one of those serious Real Conservatory student types who thinks practicing the violin until your fingers bleed is normal.

"That smells amazing," says Mei, lifting her head out of her laptop. "Will I have to talk to people?"

"Nah," says Holly, already texting Nora and Juniper to get their butts over to the house. "Keep your mouth full at all times and they can't make you socialise."

"You get me," Mei says happily. "I knew living here would work out."

They crowd around the small kitchen table in the upstairs flat: Dec and his current girlfriend Jo, Matteus, Sage, Hebe, Holly, that terrible boyfriend that Holly has been trying to break up with for three weeks now (Hebe refuses to learn his name), Mei and Mei's phone. They are halfway through their helpings of Dec's Saucy Butter Chicken, Delicious Dhal, Holy Crap That's Hot Rogan Josh, and Oops Left It In The Oven Too Long Pick Off The Burnt Bits Garlic Naan when Nora, Nora's girlfriend Vincenza, and Juniper turn up.

Lunch lasts for three hours. It's epic. When it's finally over, they all lie around groaning on beanbags in the living room, watching old Athena Owl episodes and listening to Nora report on the viewing numbers of their first Fake Geek Girl YouTube vid.

"Hey, the new season of *The Bromancers* is starting soon," says Sage. "We should rewatch the first one."

"Four hundred and twelve!" says Nora.

"Ugh," says Holly, who disapproves of *The Bromancers* because she hates fun.

Hebe smiles warmly at Dec, who is the centre of her world right now. "Any time you want to cook for us, you are more than welcome."

"Nuh uh," said Dec. "Next comfort lunch happens in your kitchen, ladies."

Hebe feels her domestic magic twitch at the thought. "I suppose…"

"Four hundred and fourteen," says Nora.

"Hebe makes a great shepherd's pie," says Sage, too sleepy to censor himself.

Because yes, she does. She used to make it all the time when he was coming over, back when they were in high school and he was her boyfriend. Usually he remembers not to refer to the relationship years, because there's still a tiny tension hanging between them that they can't quite shake.

Hebe looks for that tension right now, and can't find it. Maybe it drowned in curry.

"Sage makes a better lasagne," she mutters in retaliation.

"Feel free to prove this, both of you," volunteers Nora. "Next Saturday… Holy crap." She jack-knifes up on the couch, like she was electro-cursed. "That can't be right. Our views jumped."

"Jumped a lot," says Mei, eyes on her phone. "Is that — it's at eight hundred now."

"No way," says Sage. "There's more than eight hundred people interested in a song called Witches Roll Dice, Bitches? I thought we were niche."

"Fuck," says Nora. "Over eight fifty. Whaaat?"

"Okay," says Hebe, realising she's not going to get anything intelligible out of any of the band members for the rest of the day. "If you get to ten thousand before next Saturday, I will make you all shepherd's pie. Vegetarian AND beef."

And she does.

CHAPTER 3

NORA & JUNIPER KNOW WHEN THEY'RE NOT NEEDED

THIS ISN'T the first time that Holly derails one of their band practices with some random idea, but it's the most dramatic incident in Nora's recent memory. Here's how it happens: Holly marches in ten minutes late and announces: "I have a new song but I need to sing it to Sage first, okay?"

"Do you uh, want us to leave?" asks Juniper, which is a way more polite response than the one Nora was considering.

"Please. For like ten minutes," says Holly.

Nora is mostly impressed that Holly knows how to say 'please.' She shrugs, and grabs her bag. "We'll be at that macrobiotic muffin place on the corner. You're buying."

"Whatever," says Holly, and hands her a ten dollar note.

As Nora holds the door open for Juniper, she hears Holly say: "The working title is: You Broke My Sister's Heart With Your Big Gay Break Up And I Finally Made her Admit It, So I'm Either Going To Turn You Into A Toad Or Make You Talk About Feelings Because You're My Friend And I Can't Throw You A Damn Pride Parade Until We Clear The Air On This One."

And she hears Sage say: "Oh, fuck," like he has been expecting this horrible inevitability.

"I recognise that the title still needs work," says Holly.

"Go on, then," says Sage quietly. "Hit me."

"Walk faster," Nora urges, dragging Juniper out of there before they can hear any more.

Juniper is jittery as they sit down at the muffin place and give their orders. "I don't think I should have left Irene there with them. Last time Holly and Sage had a row, it took me three days to retune her."

"I don't think they're rowing," says Nora. "I think something cathartic is happening, which is worse. Irene would have slowed us down — better her than us." Feelings are messy. Nora is only a year and a half older than Holly and Sage but they feel like children in comparison: between them, those two have more feelings than an entire kindergarten.

Juniper looks unhappy. "I know what you're saying, but I actually like Irene better than most people, so."

They stay at the muffin place for forty minutes, with no sign of their bandmates. Nora is starting to think that Holly has straight up murdered Sage, and they are going to have to audition a new drummer.

Drumming auditions are the worst.

At the fifty minute mark, Nora's phone pings with a text:

Holly's Resting Witch Face: All Clear

Nora is So Awesome: Need us to help hide a body?

Holly's Resting Witch Face: Not this time, but I appreciate your declaration of allegiance.

Drummers Are Doofuses: You realise I'm on this group chat, babes?

Holly's Resting Witch Face: Shut up and work on that bridge for me. This is gonna be our best song yet.

Drummers Are Doofuses: Fine, but you get to tell Hebe that you wrote it.

Holly's Resting Witch Face: ...shit.

CHAPTER 4

HEBE & HOLLY ARE SUPERSTARS AT THE GAY BAR

"SEE?" says Holly, finding them a not-too-sticky table away from the loudest speakers. "This is what you need. A night out. Put yourself back out there. Gonna find you a boyf to keep you warm this winter. Or a date, at least. I know you're too goody-goody to consider a random hook up." She clinks her bottle against Hebe's. "No judgement, it's totally sweet how boring you are."

"If the point of tonight is to get me a date, why are we at a gay bar?" Hebe complains.

"Because I want to hook up with a girl tonight, obviously. Do I have to give you that speech again about how I'm eighteen and a rock singer so basically being selfish is my job?"

"No, I know that one by heart already." Hebe isn't *not* enjoying herself, though she would still rather spend her Saturday night hanging out with new flatmate Mei. Their mutual love of silence is only matched by their mutual love of Athena Owl, the best anime series of all time, and there is a new episode dropping tonight.

"Nora wants us to start a YouTube channel," says Holly. "Thoughts?"

"What does it matter what I think, Hol? It's your band."

"It always matters what you think," says Holly.

Hebe isn't listening. She is staring across the dance floor to where Sage — her Sage — is grinding and making out with another guy. Because that's a thing that happens now.

"Shit," says Holly, when she spots him. "Hebes, I'm so sorry, I had no idea he was coming here tonight. Do you want to get out of here?"

"No," says Hebe woodenly. "It's fine."

Holly sets her bottle down with a clang. "It's — Hebe. You know you don't have to be fine about this like 100% of the time, right? It's only been a few months. You can be — angry or hurt or whatever. It doesn't make you homophobic to have feelings."

"I'm not angry," says Hebe. It sounds like her voice is a long way away. "I'm — why can't I be fine? What's wrong with fine?"

Her magic, which thrives on contentment and domestic settings, gives a sickening lurch under her. Suddenly the table is clean. It feels polished under her fingertips.

Hebe gulps. Throw cushions started to appear around her. On the chairs, on the table. People will notice. Sage might detach his tongue from that random dude, turn around and see her being upset. *And the world would end.*

"I have to go," she manages, and runs for it, leaving an unexpectedly tasteful throw rug and an antique lamp on the table behind her.

She barely even realises she's crying until she finds herself sitting on the curb outside the bar, with her sister's arms wrapped around her. "I don't know why I'm even — I'm *fine*," she sobs.

"You're brilliant," Holly says into her neck. "You're perfect. Do you want me to quit?"

Hebe takes a deep, shuddering breath. It's ridiculous to fall apart like this. She has been so proud of herself for managing all this change without an emotional collapse, and here she is causing outbreaks of Better Homes and Gardens in a bar called *Sappho & Steel*. What a mess.

Also, this pavement wasn't lined with pretty flower pots when they arrived.

Holly's words finally sink in. "Quit what, quit the band? Holly, no. It's *your band*."

"I know," her sister mutters. "But — I don't have to be selfish all the time. If you need Sage to not be so up in our lives right now, I can quit. I'll be the mysterious Fake Geek Girl who left before they got famous. We can find somewhere else to live, and I can not be in the band. If it's too hard, I pick you. I'll always pick you."

Hebe has never loved her sister more. "You don't have to choose," she manages, finding a perfectly clean tissue (of course) in her pocket where there wasn't one before. She wipes her eyes. "I don't want you to choose. I *want* Sage to be all up in our lives. He's my best friend, and that hasn't changed. I won't let it change. It's not even — it's not like he cheated on me, or was mean to me. Breaking up wasn't personal. It doesn't make sense that it hurts this much."

"It doesn't have to make sense," Holly says fiercely. "I will turn him into a toad if it will make you feel better."

"No toads," says Hebe. The tissue is dry even after the third time she has wiped her eyes. Domestic magic, so useful. "Let's go home and see if we can bribe Mei away from her laptop, using devious cunning or ice cream."

"I like the way you think," says Holly. She has that look on her face, like she's plotting something, but Hebe doesn't want to know.

CHAPTER 5

HEBE KNOWS THAT JUNIPER IS GOING TO BE FINE

HEBE HAS no idea how she ended up babysitting a rock band. She's mostly stayed out of their way so far, through the auditions and rehearsals. It's good for her to get some breathing space, away from Holly and Sage, still the two points around which she constantly orbits, even in this new life of university classes and share housing.

Sage has nested in the flat upstairs, regularly clomping up and down to ask Holly about songs or amp cords or whatever. Holly is her usual whirlwind self, but Hebe has lived with her all of their lives, and this is nothing new — when Holly is in the flat, she's all noise and movement, and when she is gone it's weirdly empty.

Hebe has fallen into a kind of unspoken competition with their new flatmate Mei — when Holly is out, they test themselves for how long they can go without speaking aloud. It's glorious.

They knew each other for more than a year online, through message boards about Athena Owl's disastrous Australian spin off series, Archimedes Down Under. Hebe and Mei are the only Australians in the world who actually like that show. Legit. There's a small fandom in Japan, but even they are faintly embarrassed by the whole thing.

Hebe was worried about how they would work as flatmates IRL, but it's worked out fine, especially the non talking part.

The other day, they sat on opposite ends of the couch for two hours and when Mei got up to put the kettle on, she texted Hebe from the kitchen to see if she wanted one.

Bliss.

Anyway, the band is Holly and Sage and Nora and Juniper and NOT HEBE. That boundary has been extremely important since the whole Fake Geek Girl thing started. Until tonight.

———

IT'S their first gig playing live: three songs at the Medea's Cauldron open mic night. They are supposed to go on in fifteen minutes, but Sage is MIA, Holly started drinking early to take the edge off and is halfway to not being able to get on stage, Nora is so pissed off at Holly she is close to walking out on not just the gig but the band itself, and Juniper is having a nervous breakdown in the alley behind the pub.

Sage is not Hebe's responsibility any more. Holly is… well, Holly's always going to be her responsibility. Nora is Nora.

Juniper is the one she feels for.

So when Sage strolls in, Hebe shoves a wobbly Holly straight at him, growls "fix this" and runs after Juniper.

"I can't do this," Juniper whispers, crouching down on the back steps like she is about to throw up.

"You can," Hebe promises, patting her back gingerly. "Didn't you say you've been performing since you were six?"

"In orchestras and choirs! Not — I'm not rock and roll or indie or anything cool," Juniper gasps for air. "I'm not Holly, I can't…"

"None of us is Holly," Hebe says sharply. "That's a feature, not a bug."

Juniper stares at her, and then hiccups into laughter. "That's really mean."

"I know, right? I'm the mean sister. She's the nice one."

Juniper laughs at that too, long and hard.

Somehow, Hebe knows exactly what to say next. "Holly thinks you're rock and roll," she declares, and casts a gentle charm, one of their favourite from high school. A single lock of Juniper's hair falls out of her messy bun, glowing bright pink. Another one beside it slides down, gleaming and teal.

Hebe brushes Juniper's lower lip with her thumb, casting the lip gloss enchantment that every thirteen year old witch learns and promptly over-uses for several years.

You can go a long way on the confidence of a little lip gloss and the right person believing in you.

Juniper straightens her shoulders. "She does?"

"She definitely does," says Hebe.

Back inside, Sage sobers Holly up with another popular charm memorised by most teenagers. Nora is standing with them, game face on. Hebe delivers Juniper to them and goes to find a seat near Dec and a sulky Matteus.

Okay, fine. She's invested in the band. Whatever. That doesn't make it a structural part of her life. It's peripheral. She can give it up any time she likes.

Fake Geek Girl play three songs. The first two are pretty good, but the third… something magic happens with the third. All the ingredients come together and bang! Perfect alchemy, like Sage has been banging on about all year. Nora on keyboards, Holly on vocals, Juniper on cello, Sage on drums.

The song is kinda stupid, but catchy and full of snark. The audience loves it. The band looks like they are actually having fun.

There is wild applause and a few catcalls at the end. The band stares out at the half-full pub, red-faced and pleased with themselves. Hebe claps her hands together so hard that it hurts. Joy bubbles over as she realises she can enjoy this moment without that old sting of misery ruining things every time she looks at Sage.

I really am fine about this, she realises. *Thank goodness. It would be awful if I wasn't.*

CHAPTER 6

NESTING WITH HEBE & SAGE & HOLLY

HEBE MEETS up with her sister and her… Sage at Cirque de Cacao which is rapidly becoming their favourite haunt, two months into their first year at Belladonna University.

"So I found somewhere decent to live, finally," says Sage. "A flat-share with these two blokes, Dec and Matteus. Close to campus, and the rent's manageable. Tiny rooms — it's basically the top floor of a small house, but it's better than that shithole I'm in now." He eats two chocolate croissants off their share plate while talking.

"Bags not helping you move again," says Holly. "I'm still scraping the grunge off my shoes from last time. Hey, I found us a gig! You know that pub where we heard Kraken play the other night, Medea's Cauldron? They do an open mic night on the last Sunday of every month, to try out new bands. I signed us up for a half set, that's three songs!"

Hebe grabs the last croissant before Sage, and takes some satisfaction from biting into it. "You don't have three songs," she points out. "You've practiced the same two all summer, and you've only just figured out how to add cello to the second one."

"Time to expand our repertoire, right Sagey-boy?" Holly grins, knocking back her latte.

"Sure," says Sage, distracted. "Hey, are you two still looking for a place together?"

"The Mums have been making noises about moving out of the city before winter," says Holly. "In a word, yes. They're gonna cover some of our rent, because *such guilt* at abandoning us before we've even finished first semester."

"I've been looking," Hebe says pointedly. "And attending all my classes."

Holly pats her hand. "Some of us aren't natural multi-taskers."

"It's just, the flat under ours is up for lease," says Sage. "I know it's — but it would be great, being so close. Neighbours. Convenient for the band. If it wouldn't be weird?"

He looks at Hebe, because of course it isn't being neighbours with *Holly* that might be the weird part.

"It's fine," Hebe says automatically. "Of course it's fine. We'll check it out."

"You'd need a third," says Sage, looking relieved. Hebe feels warm, like she had passed another 'totally cool, supportive ex-girlfriend' test.

"Bags putting flyers on noticeboards!" Holly announces.

Hebe rolls her eyes at her sister. "You can't solve every problem with flyers on noticeboards, Holly."

"I give good flyer," says Holly and makes finger guns.

"I can't believe everyone thinks you're the one in the band who's *not* a nerd," Sage complains.

These two haven't changed, even as everything else changes around them. Holly and Sage being friends who kinda hate each other, that's something Hebe can hold on to.

Reassurance, like a warm blanket.

CHAPTER 7

HOLLY & SAGE & NORA HOLD AN AUDITION

"JUNIPER CRESSWELL," mumbles the cellist, the fourth student on the list for the Fake Geek Girl auditions. She glances around at the eggbox-lined garage they have hired for rehearsals.

"Not the kind of stringed instrument I was expecting," says Sage, agitated. He's been boring Holly all week with his weird rants about 'alchemy' and how putting a band together from disparate elements is somehow relevant to the magical theory he has been inhaling in his advanced first year courses and not, well. Anything to do with music, apparently.

"Shut up, it's retro," says Nora, giving Juniper a cheeky grin. "And she's cute."

"Shut up both of you and let her play!" says Holly impatiently. She can see that their banter is making Juniper nervous, and she's invested in this particular audition.

Juniper looks like she wants the stinky sound-muffling carpet to swallow her up.

But then she starts playing, eyes firmly down as she concentrates on her work. It's a cover of a 90's Madonna song, though halfway through she veers off into Queen and finishes up with a recent Kraken release, pure instrumental, making the songs sound way more ethereal and meaningful than Holly has ever thought any of them were before.

It's glorious.

"Alchemy," hums Sage knowingly, as the final notes fade.

"Fine, whatever," says Holly impatiently. "Let's see what happens when we stir the ingredients." She shoves him at his drums. "How do you feel about jamming, Juniper? See how we all mix together?"

Juniper looks startled, but then she raises her chin bravely. "Sure," she says. "If you think you can keep up with me."

Nora hoots with laughter. "I like you!"

Juniper stares expectantly at Holly, not the others.

"Right," says Holly, not used to leading as opposed to being randomly bossy and demanding. "Let's mix things up and see what goes bang."

"Yeah, now I'm remembering why you didn't take Extended Alchemy in Grade 11," Sage snarks.

But they play.

And it's… not perfect. Not yet.

But it's pretty great.

CHAPTER 8
HOLLY CATCHES A CELLIST

 WANTED: girl geek who can play stringed instrument
For songwriting, rock band shenanigans
And Taking Over the World.

HOLLY PUT a lot of work into her flyers.

She and Sage and Nora talked at length over late night drinks and early morning bacon sandwiches about what they were looking for in a fourth bandmate.

(Holly isn't convinced they need a fourth at all, but Sage and Nora say their sound needs strings of some kind and none of them are willing to pick up a guitar.)

The geek element was Holly's idea.

Nora and Sage have this superpower of creating geeky songs with surprising depth. It made Holly feel left out at first, like there wasn't a place for her in her own band...

Then Hebe named them by accident: Fake Geek Girl. It was a joke name, like the best ones always start.

Sage loved it, and it made Nora laugh. Holly found herself glowing, weirdly proud that the band was named after her. She *is* the Fake Geek Girl, and she is damn well going to own that identity.

She doesn't want other band members coming in and

stealing her spotlight. Sure, it's selfish, but she's an eighteen-year-old rock singer. Selfish comes with the job description.

The flyers are bold and bright, with a silly montage of pics Hebe took one afternoon, of Sage and Nora and Holly playing grunge dress up, pulling faces.

Holly wanted Sage to bespell the flyers to play the band's best songs-in-progress but he accidentally set fire to four of them so she did it herself, copying out the charms and applying them to the individual photocopies pages.

She missed three lectures of her first week at uni, but it was worth it. The flyers are *amaze*.

Holly posts four of them on noticeboards in the Humanities Department in the College of the Unreal before she realises she has picked up a shadow.

Every time she posts a flyer, she catches something in her peripheral vision: a swoosh of a long skirt, or a strand of hair, flicking back around the corner and out of sight.

It happens on the first floor, and the second.

"If you're so interested, you can help me put some of these up," she calls into the stairwell at one point, and hears nothing but an echo of her own voice and then a deafening silence.

Still, when they hold the open auditions a week later, Holly has that odd little non-encounter in the back of her mind. When the blushing cellist in the long floral skirt makes her apologetic way into the garage they hired for rehearsal space, Holly knows.

Hello, it's you.

CHAPTER 9

HOLLY ADDS NORA TO SAGE AND STANDS WELL BACK

HOLLY AND HEBE wait at the kitchen table. Holly's hand creeps towards the teapot again, and Hebe smacks it away. "No more tea. There is such a thing as over-hydrating."

"You are way too young to own a teapot," Holly snarks back. "It's not even your only one. You have a cupboard of them, Grandma Hallow."

Hebe raises her eyebrows and said nothing, which is hands down the most annoying thing she could possibly have done. *How is Hebe not freaked out about this?*

"What are they even talking about," Holly moans, breaking the silence after a torturous thirty seconds.

"Hopefully, musical influences they share, or this project of yours isn't going to get very far off the ground."

Holly risks a longer look at her sister. It's unfair, how difficult it is to read someone who has basically the same face. "This is okay with you, isn't it? That I'm… keeping Sage in the divorce, or whatever."

A wistful look crosses Hebe's face. "I'm keeping him too."

"He's going to be around a lot, if we pull this band together. And if you and I share a place."

Hebe holds up her phone, which has several rental ads highlighted on the screen. "Any time you have a spare hour to actually come look at flats instead of pricing drum kits with my ex-boyfriend…"

Holly flinches.

"I'm kidding," her sister says quickly. "Seriously. I'm fine, Sage and I are always going to be friends and I'm excited about your band. It's cool to see you so invested."

Holly's eyes flick to the door again. "What if they hate each other?"

"Don't all the best rock bands hate each other?" Hebe glances at the clock. "Five more minutes and then you can legitimately offer them another cuppa without looking like Stalker Girl."

Holly survives three minutes, then sidles over to stand casually in the doorway of the living room to their flat, where Sage and Nora were awkwardly introduced seventeen minutes earlier, then left alone to 'get to know each other.'

"What the fuck," Holly says flatly.

Sage and Nora are both sprawled on the floor around a… toy mountain range, covered in small metal figurines? There are dice. *Red alert, there are dice.*

"No," Hebe breathes, coming up beside her sister and nudging her with a hip. "Nora, are you into tabletop gaming?"

"I am so into it," says Nora, her eyes bright and her torn fishnets splayed across the floor. She waves a figurine. "I'm the baddest orc in the village."

"Noooo," Holly whispers in a low moan, swaying against the door frame. "She can't be. I can't have another geek in my life. We don't have the storage space."

"Best song I ever wrote is about witches playing RPGs," says Nora. "Wanna hear it later?"

"Yeah," says Sage, already clearly head over arse in platonic love with their new keyboardist. "I have one about how Neil Gaiman's novels are so mainstream it hurts."

"Sick!" says Nora.

Hebe reaches out, and pats her sister on the head sympathetically. "Remember, you were worried they might not like each other. This is better, right?"

This is so much worse.

CHAPTER 10

HOLLY'S CRISIS MANAGEMENT TECHNIQUE IS MADE OF RAINBOWS

BARS ARE NOT good places to be sad and freaked out. This one is called Sappho and Steel, a reference to something that made Hebe and Sage both laugh when they first heard it, though Holly herself never bothered to Google the joke.

Holly is on her own tonight. Her hand is actually trembling on her rainbow-coloured King Island Iced LGB-Tea, and everyone who passes her table gives her a sympathetic look, like she is some baby bisexual at her first rodeo.

She should have gone to the coffee place to have her freak out. But then, she never would have met Nora.

Nora has spiky mermaid hair, a pierced lip, and 100% all-black wardrobe. Nora volunteers as a counsellor at her local shelter. She has a hot lawyer girlfriend, and the best boots in the known universe. Nora doesn't just offer a sympathetic look, but stops by the table to check in that Holly is okay.

"I'm fine," Holly snaps.

"Sure, chook, whatever you say." There is no judgement in the stranger's voice. Holly bristles only a bit when she introduces herself and sets her spiced mead down at the table without asking.

"I'm not having a crisis," Holly adds. "At least, it's not my crisis."

Nora's eyes twinkle. "Why don't you tell me about this crisis you're not having?"

"My sister's boyfriend is gay," Holly blurts. "And that's — I mean, it's fine, obviously, I'm bi, I don't care, except it's *not* fine, because I *invested in him*, I mean we're friends but also I thought he was going to end up my brother-in-law. They don't even fight, they're perfect together except for the whole *they just broke up because he's gay* part. Now we're going off to uni and I don't even know if he'll want to come to the same one now that — I mean, I thought they were forever, you know? I'm not stupid, I know that never happens with high school boyfriends, but it was totally going to happen with them."

So that was a speech and a half. She's outed herself as barely out of high school twice over, and she doesn't even care about that because Nora probably isn't going to want to sleep with her anyway.

(She doesn't know about the hot lawyer girlfriend yet but when she finds that part out, well, of course Nora is taken, because Nora is the best of everything.)

"How's your sister taking it?" Nora asks, sipping her drink.

"That's the worst part," Holly snarls. "She's *fine*. I mean, she's sad, but she doesn't blame him. She hasn't even got angry about it. I broke furniture when I found out. Like, for 24 hours I thought I had to hate him, but she doesn't want me to, and… it's just weird, you know? He's like family and. Ugh. Would it be weird to start a rock band with him so we still have an excuse to hang out?"

Nora has the kind of face you tell things to, apparently. Holly didn't even know that was going to come out of her mouth.

"I don't think it's weird," says Nora. And then: "Do you need someone on keyboards?"

CHAPTER 11

SAGE & HEBE ARE TOTALLY GOING TO BE FINE

HEBE WAS NOT EXPECTING Sage on her doorstep today. Or this weekend, actually. She has family stuff, and shopping to do, and university forms to fill in. They have the whole summer to hang out, and don't need to be in each other's back pockets all the time. So…?

She certainly wasn't expecting her boyfriend to be red in the face and breathing hard like he just ran across the length of the city to get to her. His magic, which is ridic powerful but doesn't usually react to her gentle, non-threatening domestic charms, sparks violently against her like a weaponised sunburn. He is agitated; upset.

"Sage, what's wrong?"

"I think I'm gay," he blurts out.

Hebe has a moment in which she thinks absolutely nothing. Then it catches up with her.

"Um, okay," she manages.

"I'm so sorry."

Somehow she gets him inside. She makes him a cuppa, almost without thinking — her wretched housewife magic takes over, wanting to be a good hostess. That calms any more panicky thoughts in her brain. They sit on the ugly couch that her Mums adore so much. Hebe resists the urge to hug him because do they even do that now?

Not being able to hug Sage is scarier than the thought of him not being attracted to her. Sage not actually being all that attracted to her physically is something Hebe has been aware of for a long time, like white noise. It literally never occurred to her before this moment that it wasn't her fault.

What were they now?

"Thank you for telling me?" she manages. What she does not say is 'actually this explains a lot.' She will save those thoughts for later, when she debriefs with Holly.

Because. Actually. *This explains a lot.*

She's going to have to tell Holly. She's going to have to tell everyone. She's going to be unpacking this for *weeks*.

Sage is wrecked. "I haven't been lying to you, I promise, babe. I literally just figured this out today."

How? Hebe wants to ask, but that part is none of her business, probably.

Three years. They have been dating for nearly three years, from the beginning of Grade 10 through to right now, and they've been *fine*. What makes today different?

"When you say gay," she says after a moment. "You don't mean bi, or… because that would be completely okay, of course."

"Nope," he says, staring at the floor. "Which. Yeah. Sorry. That would have been better. But no."

She's weirdly calm. She doesn't burst into tears. That's good, right? She can handle this. She can be chill and supportive. No drama. "So is this where we break up?"

Sage looks at her, panic in his face. "I — I think so? I don't want to lose you, Hebes. You're still. You're my best person, you know? I love you."

Hebe takes the cup from him, sets it on the table out of the way, and lets herself hug him after all. Sage's arms around her felt as they always have, safe and warm. Easy. Uncomplicated. "You won't lose me. It's going to be fine. We'll figure this out."

Fine. That was one word for it.

CHAPTER 12
SAGE FIGURES SOMETHING OUT

HIS NAME WAS Isaac but we'd been referring to him as Iago behind his back because... well, Holly has a type, and it's basically 'handsome, borderline criminal, possibly has a part-time job as a Disney villain.' If she was dating him, chances were high he was a sketchy dude.

And she was. Dating him. Which made this like, 400% worse.

Holly's romantic tastes are... well, she has her own special version of the binary. She gets crushes on these amazing, competent, intelligent, mostly unattainable women, but somehow she always settles for the good looking douchey dudes who make her feel pretty and treat her like crap.

So Isaac/Iago was a douche, and pretentious with it, all floppy black hair and intense eye contact. He had to be using vanity charms, no way those emerald eyes of his were legit.

I hated him on sight.

He reckoned he was a in a band, but they never had gigs or even practice except when he wanted to get out of plans he'd made with Holly.

He could play literally two chords, but carried his guitar everywhere with him like it was the Holy Fucking Grail. He flirted with everything that moved. I swear I once saw him hitting on a tree.

Even his magic was irritating, all hot and abrasive. It clashed badly with mine, brought me out in a sweat when he was nearby. At least, I thought it was his magic.

Yeah. I was behind the eight-ball on this one. Slower than dirt.

This isn't a story that does me any favours, by the way, though it was never gonna be. Feel free to skip to the end.

So I walked in on Asshole Iago making time with some emo sales guy behind the counter of the new hipster music store Vinyl Is Back, Baby.

Like, what the fuck? Right out there in the open. Holly's like a sister to me which I guess is some excuse for why I grabbed him by his stupid high-collared shirt and shoved him off into the alley out the back to scare the shit out of him.

My magic blistered out of me and his charged back at me in a sonic wave that felt like all kinds of challenge.

"It wasn't anything that mattered," the green-eyed pretty boy drawled at me, like I was the one screwing up here. "C'mon Sage, don't be so uptight. I just blow the dude sometimes and he gives me a discount on new releases. That's not cheating, it's a good deal."

"Holly know about your arrangement?" I growled at him.

"Of course not, I'm not stupid." He leaned against the wall, supremely confident that I wasn't going to hit him. His eyes lidded in a lazy expression, and he looked me up and down. "You don't have to be stupid either. Holly's a sweet girl, neither of us want her feelings to be hurt. Keep your mouth shut, and I'll make it worth your while."

When I realised what he was offering — hell, he was five seconds from dropping to his knees right there in the alley — white hot rage surged through me. I almost punched him in the face, that's how much of a redneck cliche I am deep down, I guess.

That wasn't the worst part. The worst was the coil of want that unspooled for a moment. A fierce, angry, completely hot desire to shove him against a wall and… yeah, hitting him wasn't actually what I wanted to do right then.

He saw it. That was the worst part. (That wasn't the worst part, obviously, but I had a whole lot of repression and denial to unpack before I got to the actual worst part.) He smiled, like he'd proved something. "I knew you'd been watching me."

Had I? That didn't make any sense. But right now, nothing made sense.

"Tell her or I will," I managed to say, then turned and walked away.

After half a block, I started to run.

Why did it have to be that guy?

Embarrassing as hell, that despite having the world's best girlfriend, I somehow managed to share Holly's terrible taste in men?

Also.

Shit.

Hebe.

I had a lot of thinking to do, now the adrenaline was starting to wear off.

Because the truth was.

Yeah.

It wasn't just that guy.

This wasn't new.

And that right there was the worst part, rolling out in front of me like the shittiest red carpet in the history of the world. I was going to have to tell her.

Right now.

It couldn't wait.

CHAPTER 13

HEBE FLIES BETTER THAN HOLLY

"You're welcome," Holly said smugly.

The sisters were running broomstick drills, less than a metre above the school oval. Grade 10 had just started, and there was an option to start training for your provisional flying licence before you turned sixteen.

Hebe had hoped her twin could manage at least one lap without falling off, before they went for the test. It wasn't looking good.

"I have a boyfriend now, Holly," she said with a roll of her eyes. "It has literally nothing to do with you."

"If I'd dated Sage when he first got to this school, you would not be with him now. Right? So, you're welcome."

"I'm not giving you credit for this."

"He's a huge nerd, even if he does have cool taste in music sometimes. You two are perfect for each other."

"Yes," Hebe said crisply. "I'm aware."

"So you're…"

"I will push you off your broom."

Holly laughed so hard she fell off her broom anyway.

CHAPTER 14

SAGE LEARNS A SURPRISING
FACT ABOUT HEBE HALLOW

THERE WERE four of them in the Mundane Reality gaming club. Sage wasn't sure if it was worth getting invested in a card game about a world without magic — that summed up the first thirteen years of his life, and it was boooring. But his aunt was making noises about him needing friends, and it was this or sign up for some kind of sport.

Weevil and Lam were all right, the kind of speccy kids that Sage always got along with as long as he remembered to act less threatening than his wide frame and natural resting thug face implied. Once he passed their tests of hidden geek knowledge and made it known that he was willing to push over any arsehole who looked at them funny, they accepted him as one of their own.

Sage was playing the long game here. He was determined to get these kids playing old school tabletop D&D by the end of the term. With actual fucking dragons, thank you very much.

The club consisted of Weevil, Lam, Sage and Hebe, the only girl, who had so many school commitments that she only ever made it to one in three of their sessions.

"I don't get her," Sage complained, after his milkman character was trapped in a traffic jam for four turns. "Sometimes she's totes cool about gaming and comics and music and whatever. We can talk for hours — she's read every Terry Pratchett novel and she knows obscure indie bands I've never heard of, right? But other times I start a conversation and she just looks at me with this blank expression like she has no idea what words mean. Is there some kind of memory curse fad going around or something? Because I've heard about some of the weird things that happen at magic schools in the big city…"

Weevil and Lam stared at each other, and then back to him.

"Bro," said Weevil, and then stopped.

"You know they're twins, right?" said Lam. "Holly and Hebe Hallow. I mean, you hang out with them a lot. You have to know. Hebe's the one who comes to the club sometimes, knows about books and gaming. Holly's the crazy one who's into like, guitars and bands and shit."

Sage froze for about three seconds. "Yeah," he said, laughing it off. "Obviously I know they're twins. I was just kidding."

Weevil cracked up first, and then Lam. "You so weren't kidding."

"This is amazing."

"HOW COULD YOU NOT HAVE FIGURED OUT THEY WERE TWO SEPARATE PEOPLE?"

"Guys," Sage said urgently. "They must never know. You gotta take this one to your graves."

CHAPTER 15

HOLLY SPOTS A CUTE BOY

"HE'S MINE," said Holly, when she spied the new boy across the canteen. "Look at those shoulders. Very promising."

Hebe didn't even turn to look around. "You can't dibs people, Holly. Anyway, I thought you were swearing off boys."

"Not cute ones, obviously," said Holly. "Poor dear looks so grumpy and lost. Shall I invite him to sit with us?"

"No," hissed Hebe, but it was too late.

Holly was already flitting across the canteen floor.

Hebe had an Alchemy test up next with the most sarcastic and demanding teacher in the school. That was totally the reason she didn't stick around to watch Holly hit on the new boy with the great shoulders.

Yep, that was the only reason.

———

TWO DAYS LATER, Sage McClaren had accidentally blown up the school laboratory three times, and made it rain frogs out of the fire sprinklers, because apparently he had more magic than any human being who had ever lived and never learned even an iota of control because of his weird religious upbringing.

Hebe looked over at his open, laughing face and thought:

Yes. Okay. If can you still have a sense of humour in the face of that level of disaster? I probably want to be friends with you.

THE END
BUT ALSO THE BEGINNING

ABOUT THE AUTHOR

Tansy Rayner Roberts is an award-winning Australian science fiction and fantasy author who owns far too pointy hats. She had a great time at university.

- Listen to Tansy on Sheep Might Fly, a podcast where she reads aloud her stories as audio serials. The Belladonna U series started here!
- Read Tansy's stories before anyone else when you pledge to her Patreon: patreon.com/tansyrr
- What tea is Tansy drinking? Find out when you subscribe to her excellent newsletter.
- Follow Tansy on Amazon or Bookbub so you never miss a release.

facebook.com/TansyRRoberts
twitter.com/tansyrr
instagram.com/tansyrr

HOLIDAY BREW
(BELLADONNA U #2)

What's an Aussie witch to do for Halloween when the weather is all spring sunshine and happiness? What's the appropriate ritual for breaking up with your boyfriend on the Summer Solstice? Who did Ferd Chauvelin kiss on New Year's Eve?

Follow our Belladonna U student witches: Sage, Hebe, Juniper, Viola and their friends through three holiday festivals with their usual romantic disasters, friendship dramas, and magical explosions.

(Includes the stories Halloween Is Not A Verb, Solstice on the Rocks and Kissing Basilisks)

Get your copy today!

Turn the page for a sneak peek of the first chapter of *Holiday Brew*.

HALLOWEEN IS NOT A VERB
CHAPTER 1: MISTAKES ARE MADE

Viola Vale had made a crucial error.

As a postgrad student, it wasn't unusual to be asked to run a tutorial group for first years. When her department asked her to volunteer, she signed right up. That was perfectly reasonable. It didn't even count as a bad life choice.

When she realised she had actually been handed a third year Advanced Course, that was when she should have said no. Teaching students her own age was bound to lead to trouble, and she knew it even as she ummed and erred.

But, as Professor M said blithely, who would be better qualified to take seminars on The Magical Application of Ancient Myth?

(Apart from Professor M herself, a lowkey genius and qualified expert in the field, who clearly had her own reasons for not wanting to run this class)

Yes, it was relevant to her thesis, and yes Viola could talk through the course content in her sleep.

So yes, she said yes.

Big mistake.

Third year advanced students meant Jules Nightshade and Sage McClaren, who had both independently decided to take this class despite it not being remotely relevant for either of their majors. The bastards.

Both men were brilliant, with abilities and intelligence far beyond their peers. Both were being fast-tracked for postgraduate work themselves, once they graduated later this year, though Jules had yet to commit to that; he had a lot of job offers.

Both men technically counted as friends, she supposed, though she went back and forth as to whether Sage counted as a mate now, or a frenemy one stolen band t-shirt away from being her nemesis. Jules had been Viola's ride-or-die BFF for most of her life; there was no escaping him now.

Both men were arseholes.

That wasn't even the worst part.

The worst part was, they still wanted to bang each other. This class gave her a front row seat for all the sexual tension, passive aggressive flirting, academic one-upmanship, and the magical equivalent of shaking tail feathers.

Right now, Sage and Jules were having the most offensively intense discussion about the Icarus myth from across the circle of chairs, apparently forgetting there was anyone else in the room.

The other students in the tutorial watched the two of them with a fascination that bordered on the perverse, some of them discreetly taking notes on Sage and Jules' increasingly outlandish theories. At least Viola was here to witness this, and would know what was up if the mid-semester essays all repeated the obnoxious proposal that the source of beeswax for Icarus' wings was in any way significant to the mythic narrative.

One student had a laptop balanced precariously across her thighs, typing madly. Viola was pretty sure she was writing fanfic.

Sage was red in the face. This often happened when he was anywhere near Jules. Jules himself had gone all cold and sarcastic. Frost crackled across his eyebrows.

The student's laptop made a small fritzing sound as the magic tensions in the room — from Sage, probably, though Jules wasn't helping — reached their zenith.

"Okay, we're stopping there," Viola said briskly. "You have to decide on your final practical project by next week, including group selection, or I'll pick a topic and a partner for you. I need an abstract covering the myth you intend to explore, and the relevant spellwork you'll be engaging in. Also an ethics statement if that spellwork involves living creatures — which yes, does include human subjects. We'll use next week's tutorial to cover Minoan symbolism, so read the last three chapters of *The Circead*." She pointed a finger at Sage. "You need to go drink a cup of coffee right the hell now."

"Sorry," he said with that wide, horrendously charming grin of his. He gave Jules a restrained bro nod which wasn't fooling anyone, and hurried out of the room.

Jules leaned back in his chair like he had nowhere else to be.

"You," Viola said impatiently, after the last of the students filed out. "Seriously, Jules?"

"Seriously what?"

"I thought—" and she checked herself briefly, because her department was relaxed about some things, but she should probably be careful what she might be overheard saying to a student. "I thought he was out of your system," she said finally, in a mutter.

"I have no idea what you're talking about, Vale," said Jules, entirely innocent.

"You're buying lunch," she grumbled.

READ THE REST IN *Holiday Brew*.